# A Pemberley Medley

### Short stories by
### Abigail Reynolds

Intertidal Press

Published by Intertidal Press, 700 Rayovac Drive, Suite 220, Madison, WI 53711
www.pemberleyvariations.com

To Rena with love,
for cheering me on when I needed it
and for a lifetime of sisterly support and affection

## Also by Abigail Reynolds

WHAT WOULD MR. DARCY DO?

MR. DARCY'S OBSESSION

TO CONQUER MR. DARCY
(previously published as *Impulse & Initiative*)

THE MAN WHO LOVED PRIDE AND PREJUDICE
(previously published as *Pemberley by the Sea*)

MR. FITZWILLIAM DARCY: THE LAST MAN IN THE WORLD

MR. DARCY'S UNDOING – *coming October 2011*
(previously published as *Without Reserve*)

BY FORCE OF INSTINCT

# Table of Contents

# *Intermezzo*

*This is my first short story and still one of my favorites. It was also my first time as a writer struggling with the dilemma of whether to allow a deliberate historical discrepancy to sneak in. For plot purposes, the wedding breakfast had to be a sit-down meal instead of the customary stand-up affair. Fortunately for me, a knowledgeable reader pointed out that Bingley was from Northern England where sit-down wedding breakfasts were the norm, so you'll just have to assume that he decided to bring the custom with him for his own wedding.*

ELIZABETH GAZED AT her reflection in the mirror, wondering if the changes of the last year showed in her face as much as she felt them in her heart. Today was a day full of memories. The last time she had prepared for a ball at Netherfield, she had taken more than usual care with her appearance in hopes of winning Wickham's heart. Now she was thankful he had never made an appearance, preventing her from making an even greater fool of herself than she had managed without his presence.

This ball would be quite different, and her preparations had not been elaborate. All eyes would be on Jane at the ball, and Elizabeth had no one to impress with her beauty. There would be no Mr. Wickham and no Mr. Darcy tonight. How blind she had been, to believe the one and scorn the other, and not to recognize the attentions Mr. Darcy had been paying her for what they were!

A familiar feeling of guilt settled over her at the thought of Darcy. Her shame over her infamous treatment of him at

Hunsford had only increased during the intervening months. It began after Mr. Bingley's sudden reappearance at Netherfield in May. Anxious over the prospect of encountering Mr. Darcy again after their embarrassing parting in Kent, Elizabeth had asked Bingley on his first visit to Longbourn whether his friend intended to join them.

The look of concern which had crossed that gentleman's face had been unmistakable. *No, unfortunately, he will not, although I invited him; he is not of a sociable bent these days,* he had said. *He is in a very black humour; no one knows why, but he has closeted himself away and does not even receive callers. I have only seen him once myself, when he called on me to tell me....to give me some intelligence that he thought I might find useful.* Bingley had glanced at Elizabeth with an embarrassed smile then, allowing her some hint as to what that information might have been, and how it might have related to his abrupt return to Hertfordshire. *I have never seen him look so ill - I hope his spirits recover soon; he is the best of men, and I hate to see him in such distress.*

She had known that he must have been disappointed by her refusal, but she had not thought that, given the level of reservations he had expressed in his proposal, he would find much difficulty in overcoming his affections. The discovery that she had the power to cause him such suffering was a sobering one, the more so as she spent more time in Bingley's company, as Jane's chaperone, and heard his stories which often enough included Darcy, always in a most favourable light. It was clear that he thought Darcy to be the soul of generosity, thoughtfulness, and cleverness, a view which quite contradicted that which Elizabeth had held.

When, in due course, Bingley and Jane became engaged, Bingley made a trip to London to arrange matters with his attorney and to settle some business. On his return, he was in as much of a temper as Elizabeth had ever seen him. As usual, she had been in the background when he talked to Jane, his voice raised in anger perhaps louder than he realized. *I told him of our engagement, and he congratulated me and seemed to speak with sincere pleasure at the news; but then when I asked him to stand up with me at our wedding, he refused! He said that business would not permit him to leave London, as if I would believe such an excuse. It is only half a morning's travel, and two months away - how could he possibly be too busy? I was hurt, but I remained civil, and expressed my hope that he would at least be able to attend our wedding, and he said that he thought even that unlikely to be possible. I grew angry, then, and accused him of disapproving of my choice, which he adamantly denied, saying that once he might have taken ....other considerations in mind, but now he thought differently, and was nothing but delighted that I was taking this step. And when I pressed him again to come, he turned away and said, 'Bingley, you do not know what you are asking,' and then he went so far as to ask me to leave! I would never have thought it of him; I have misjudged him badly in thinking him a good friend.* Jane, with a glance at Elizabeth, had placed her hand on his arm to stop him at that point, but the damage had been done.

It had been difficult for her to forgive herself after that, to know that her cruelty towards him had been such that he would risk ending a long and valued friendship solely to avoid having to see her again. She had vowed to herself that never again would she allow herself to give in to her anger and to treat anyone so harshly.

Since there was nothing she could do to make amends, she resolved to try to put it from her mind. Her northern tour with her aunt and uncle had provided a distraction, at least until Mrs. Gardiner had taken it into her head to visit Pemberley. Hearing such a different and complimentary view of Mr. Darcy from his housekeeper and seeing the care with which the estate was run could not help but leave her with a warmer feeling about the man himself, and an odd feeling of loss that she had never had the occasion to know that part of him.

She sighed as her mind came back to the present. There was nothing to be done for it now. The opportunity would not return again, and she could not undo the past. Resolving, as she had so many times already, to think no more of it, she went to Jane's room to see if she needed any assistance with her preparations.

The drawing-room at Netherfield was crowded with people, all older and more assured than she, it seemed; ordinarily it was a scene that would have raised a great deal of anxiety in Georgiana, but she had come to Hertfordshire with a goal in mind, and this ball offered her best opportunity to achieve it. She had needed to beg for permission to attend, which was granted only on the condition that she would dance with no one except Mr. Bingley and any men whom he specifically introduced to her with that intent, a compromise that Bingley hoped would be satisfactory to Darcy. Dancing was not on her mind, however. She was engaged in a dually unpleasant task: meeting as many people as possible in as short a time as possible, a job highly unsuited to one as shy as she, and employing the person best able to help her in that effort, no matter how distasteful her company might be. Miss Bingley knew more of the company than anyone else present, and was willing to devote her time to pleasing Miss Darcy.

The one person Georgiana had been happy to meet so far was Mr. Bingley's betrothed. Miss Bennet was everything that was lovely and gentle, and could not have looked happier. Unfortunately, Georgiana had so far had a notable lack of success in reaching her true goal. She was determined to discover the woman her brother was breaking his heart over, to find her and to acquaint herself with her, and then to use her knowledge to help her brother move past his infatuation. She had very little information to help her in identifying the mysterious woman - from her brother's reaction to the idea of attending this wedding,

Georgiana was certain it was someone who would be in attendance at the ceremony, and likely at the ball as well. She would naturally have to be young and attractive, and presumably married, for why else would Fitzwilliam not simply ask her to marry him? No woman in her right mind would refuse him. She had a suspicion as to her first name, from overhearing her brother say despairingly, "Elizabeth" when he had thought he was alone and had touched the brandy decanter a little too heavily.

She was beginning to feel as if far too many people lived in Hertfordshire, but determinedly continued to ask Miss Bingley to introduce her to as many as possible.

Elizabeth was not formed for ill-humour, and it did not take her long to recover her spirits once she arrived at the ball and was no longer subject to Lydia's complaints of how many more balls she would have been able to attend if only she had been allowed to go to Brighton. There were a number of people present who were strangers to her, friends and family of Mr. Bingley who had come to attend the wedding. Bingley introduced her to Mr. Ansfield, who would be groomsman at the wedding, and the gentleman asked the honour of her hand for the next two dances. He proved to be a very entertaining partner who regaled her with outrageous and amusing ideas of how he might disgrace himself during the wedding service, which problems he had given serious consideration to since he was to be married himself in some months. She was sorry to relinquish his company, but had also been asked to dance by several gentlemen of her acquaintance. Although she found this a pleasurable pastime, by the end of the third set she was ready to seek some refreshment. She was feeling more than a little lonely; she was accustomed to spending time at such occasions talking to Jane, or formerly to Charlotte, but tonight her sister was the center of attention and Charlotte was long gone.

Deciding that she might as well pay her respects to the official hostess of the occasion, she approached Miss Bingley with a compliment on the entertainment. "Miss Bingley, it is a pleasure to see you once more," she said politely.

"It is a very happy occasion," Miss Bingley replied smoothly. "Miss Bennet, may I introduce you to Miss Darcy? Miss Darcy, this is Miss Elizabeth Bennet; it is her sister who is marrying my brother."

Elizabeth was quite taken by surprise to discover Miss Darcy's presence; and with a moment of panic, thinking the sister unlikely to travel without her brother, she scanned the room for a tall, dark figure. Realizing that Miss Darcy was looking at her with a penetrating gaze, she drew her attention back and expressed her pleasure in making the acquaintance. She could not help but feel flustered, and was certain that her cheeks were betraying her embarrassment on the occasion, although she knew that neither of the others were likely to be acquainted with the details of her history with Mr. Darcy. "I have heard a great deal about you from Miss Bingley, as well as from your brother, Miss Darcy," she said. "I understand that you are a fine musician."

"They have no doubt been far too kind to me," said Georgiana gravely, wondering if this young woman could possibly be the one she was seeking. The name was correct, and she was apparently acquainted with him, but she was unmarried, which made it seem unlikely. Still, it was worth pursuing; if nothing else, Miss Bennet might provide leads as to who else her brother was acquainted with in Hertfordshire. "You are acquainted with my brother, then?"

"Yes, I met him when he visited Netherfield last autumn," said Elizabeth. "Is he here this evening?" She could not help but ask the question directly.

"No, unfortunately, business requires him to remain in London," said Georgiana.

Miss Bingley, feeling that this was quite enough of an acquaintance for her taste between Miss Darcy and Eliza Bennet of the fine eyes, said, "There was a slight acquaintance, it is true, from when you visited here when your sister was ill."

Elizabeth, feeling the implication, could not resist making a response. "Yes, it was but slight, though I had the pleasure of meeting him again some months later when I visited Kent. I was frequently in company there with him and his cousin, Colonel Fitzwilliam, while they were visiting Lady Catherine de Bourgh. So you see, I have quite a list of people who have told me of your prowess at the pianoforte, Miss Darcy; it was a common topic of conversation at Rosings."

This intelligence of Miss Bennet's apparent intimacy with Mr. Darcy's family clearly came as an unpleasant surprise to Miss Bingley, who chose to insert herself at that moment with a paean of praise for Miss Darcy's abilities. Georgiana, who as a rule disliked the attention such compliments brought, for once was grateful, as it gave her the opportunity to collect her thoughts. She realized with excitement that she had indeed found her quarry - it was directly after his visit to Rosings that her brother had sunk into his gloom, not to mention that as sister of the bride, she would be quite unavoidable at Mr. Bingley's wedding. This *must* be her; why, then, was there a difficulty? Perhaps she was promised to someone else?

Miss Darcy somehow forced herself to continue an active conversation to maintain Miss Bennet's interest. *Fitzwilliam would be proud of me if he were to see how outgoing I am being!* she thought with a touch of irony, since it was only for his sake she was overcoming her native shyness. Luck seemed to favor her tonight, and a gentleman came to claim Miss Bingley's hand for the next dance, leaving her alone with Elizabeth.

"It is a shame my brother could not be here tonight; I am sure that he would enjoy renewing his acquaintance with everyone he met here," Georgiana offered tentatively, looking for a way to raise the question.

Elizabeth was discovering that she was both longing to ask about Mr. Darcy and afraid of what she might hear. "Yes, Mr. Bingley was very disappointed that he could not be in attendance," she said by way of compromise.

"Mr. Bingley has been a very dear friend of his for some years, and I know my brother is sorry to miss his wedding, but the truth is that he has been very little in company of late," Georgiana said, watching Elizabeth closely.

She felt a slight stab of pain at her words. "He must be quite busy, then," she attempted.

"Not so busy, no," said Georgiana slowly. "But he has not been himself for some months."

Elizabeth found it suddenly hard to breathe. Surely he could not still be in such pain as that! "He has not been ill, I hope?"

"No, his health has been excellent as always - I believe it is more an unhappiness which afflicts him, but he is not one to confide in a much younger sister." Georgiana could hardly credit what she was saying, speaking of such personal matters to a complete stranger, yet she knew as if by instinct that Elizabeth was somehow intimately involved in this.

For her part, Elizabeth was uncertain if she could bear to hear any more of this. She did not wish him to suffer; she knew that he did not deserve such suffering; and although she was the cause, she had no way of offering him relief. "I am sorry to hear that," she said uncomfortably. "Please give him my best regards, when next you see him."

"I will be happy to do so," Georgiana replied. *You have no idea of how careful I will be to do exactly that!* she thought. "Your sister is very lovely; I have always wished to have a sister," she added.

"And I have four!" exclaimed Elizabeth with a laugh, glad for the change of subject.

"Four? And are they all married?" Georgiana asked, intending to gather as much information as possible.

"No, none, Jane is the eldest, and first of us to reach the altar. All the rest of us are at home, and like to remain that way for some time," said Elizabeth. She pointed out her younger sisters to Miss Darcy, who seemed quite inordinately curious about them. No doubt it was interesting to her to glimpse a family so different from her own. Elizabeth found her a subject almost as interesting; she had heard at Lambton that Miss Darcy was exceedingly proud, consistent with Wickham's description of her; yet her manners were unassuming and gentle, and if she still possessed some of the awkwardness of her age, it seemed bridged by amiability. She was grateful to discover Miss Darcy did not seem to be the acute and unembarrassed observer her brother was.

Georgiana managed to attach herself quite firmly to Elizabeth, much to the displeasure of Miss Bingley, who had never heard her utter so many words in their entire acquaintance. Elizabeth was amused by Miss Bingley's discomfiture, but had some reservations about encouraging the friendship of Miss Darcy; she did not think Mr. Darcy likely to be pleased were his sister to return to London with news of her particular acquaintance.

She had not reckoned with Miss Darcy's determination; she somehow convinced Mr. Bingley to allow her to accompany him on his visit to Longbourn the next day. Though Elizabeth tried to encourage her to talk to Mary or Kitty as being closer to her own age and also not as likely to incur the discomfort of her brother should their names ever be mentioned, Miss Darcy seemed to lapse into being tongue-tied and shy whenever she was not speaking directly to Elizabeth. After Mr. Bingley made a reference to her habitual timidity, Elizabeth began to wonder with some amusement what odd fate had given her this strange ability to attract members of the Darcy family. Although she found Georgiana's company to be pleasant, she was not sad that their acquaintance would have to terminate immediately upon Jane's marriage, given the pain which would inevitably follow any closer association between them.

The day of the wedding came quickly. The wedding ceremony was both solemn and joyful; Jane was as beautiful as a bride could be, and Bingley could not stop smiling. Elizabeth, standing at the front of the church, felt all happiness on her sister's behalf, and reflected that here was one good thing which had come out of that dreadful day at Hunsford: Jane and Bingley, together as they should be. She thought with appreciation of Darcy, who had triumphed over himself sufficiently to give them this opportunity, and she felt proud of him.

Elizabeth followed the new Mr. and Mrs. Bingley down the aisle after the ceremony, her hand on Mr. Ansfield's arm. With a contagious smile, he said to her playfully, "I hope Bingley appreciates it that I made it through without disgracing myself."

"You did beautifully," she replied with a happy laugh, placing her free hand lightly on his arm for a moment. "I am certain that Mr. Bingley was quite pleased; that is, if he was able to notice anything at all beyond my sister!"

They were almost to the doors of the church when she let her gaze move over the assembled guests, stopping abruptly with shock when it came to a pair of dark eyes which she would never forget. The look in them was one she had never seen before, though - one of cold distaste which seemed to cut straight through her. All her happiness in the day seemed to vanish as though it had never been, and was replaced by a wrenching pain.

She forced herself to look away, although some part of her wanted to fix her eyes on him forever. Relying on Mr. Ansfield to guide her outside, she somehow managed to carry on, greeting guests, kissing Jane, and embracing Bingley, but all the while her thoughts were on Darcy. She had imagined meeting him again so many times; she had imagined being faced with pain and even anger, but she had never thought she would see loathing in his eyes, and the thought of it cut her like a knife. She could not say that she did not deserve it, but it pained her.

She was unusually quiet on the carriage ride to Netherfield, but fortunately this passed notice as her mother reviewed the triumphs of the wedding in detail. Elizabeth could not help thinking on the power of her reaction to seeing Darcy once more, and in so unexpected a manner. The wedding breakfast was likely to be a trial; she could not decide whether she more hoped for the chance to speak to him or dreaded it. Regardless of his behaviour, she was determined to meet him with the utmost civility as befitted a man of honour and sense whom she had wronged. Perhaps then she would at least have the comfort of knowing that he would no longer believe she thought badly of him.

On their arrival, Elizabeth found Jane surrounded by a cluster of well-wishers. Bingley was off to one side, talking urgently to the butler about some matter. She did not wish under the circumstances to stand by herself, so she sought out a friendly face. Spotting Mr. Ansfield across the room, she was about to move in his direction when Miss Darcy appeared by her side.

"Miss Bennet!" cried the girl. "You shall never guess - my brother has come, after all. He was planning to return to London directly after the ceremony, but I begged him to stay for the breakfast, as did Mr. Bingley, and he finally agreed."

"You must be very pleased to see him," Elizabeth responded, her own heart too heavy for good cheer.

"I am - and you must come say hello to him; he knows so few people here, and you know, I am sure, how shy he is of making new acquaintances."

Elizabeth could scarcely refuse this request, but she was taken aback by Miss Darcy's words. Shy? It was not a concept she had ever thought to apply to Darcy of all people, yet it made many things plain to her, from why he had refused to dance with her at the assembly to the silences she had interpreted as pride. With some anxiety, she followed the girl across the room, thinking it might be as well to accomplish this first meeting, no matter how it should go.

"Fitzwilliam, you remember Miss Bennet, do you not? She has told me of making your acquaintance here," said Georgiana with determined cheerfulness. She had no intention of allowing this opportunity to pass by, whether for good or ill, and it was her last chance to discover what lay between her brother and Miss Bennet.

Elizabeth felt almost helplessly drawn to look at him. He was a little thinner than she had recalled, but otherwise appeared much the same. The hostility she had perceived in the church seemed to be gone, or at least well disguised; he now appeared only impenetrably grave.

He did not seem much at ease, but he made her his compliments with civility, enquiring after those members of her family he had not yet had the pleasure to see that day. She hardly knew how to reply, whether to respond to the alteration in his civility since they had last met, or to the severity of his countenance. She temporized briefly with a few words on the subject of the wedding, then said, "I had been given to understand that you were not expected here today, sir. I know it must be a great pleasure to Mr. Bingley and my sister that you were able to be in attendance."

"The pleasure is mine, Miss Bennet," he said with more than a touch of irony in his voice.

Elizabeth's smile faltered for a moment at the implication, but she was determined to be civil no matter what provocation she was offered. "Your sister tells me that business has been keeping you in Town, Mr. Darcy. Is it very quiet there at this season?"

"It is quiet enough; I am not there for my entertainment," he said coolly. He wondered how she would react if he said that he was in London because he could not face going to Pemberley without her, at least not once Bingley had decided to return to Netherfield instead of taking up his invitation to visit Derbyshire. But there was no point in even wondering what she would think; he had seen how the very sight of him wiped the smile from her face in the church, and he knew that she would not be speaking with him now had Georgiana not forced them into this position. What ill fortune that of all the people in Hertfordshire, Georgiana should choose to attach herself to *her*! She was looking at him playfully, and he could see he was to fall victim to some of the teasing that had so enchanted him. He steeled himself to bear it.

"It was quite a surprise when Mr. Bingley returned to Netherfield in the spring, Mr. Darcy. You were very sly; you did not mention a word of it when you were in Kent," she said.

*Touché, Miss Bennet,* he thought. With the faintest of smiles, he said aloud, "I was not aware of it at the time. As you know, Mr. Bingley is a creature of impulse at times, so it did not come as a surprise to me when he decided to return. I understand as well that the regiment has left Meryton." He was not averse to handing back her challenge.

She coloured slightly. "I am relieved to say that is accurate, sir," she said, "although unfortunately not all of my family is in agreement with my views on the matter."

*So she did believe what I told her in my letter; that is something, at least,* he thought. It was good to know he had been acquitted of cruelty in that regard, at least. He tried to think of a response, but there seemed to be an embargo on every subject. Before the silence could become too awkward, however, Elizabeth excused herself, claiming she was needed by her mother. He bowed silently, a familiar feeling of emptiness settling back on his heart as he watched her walk away.

"Miss Bennet is very charming," said Georgiana with determined good cheer. "I like her very much."

Darcy's face twisted in an ironic half-smile. "Yes, she is charming," he said shortly. The last thing he wanted at the moment was to listen to Georgiana singing Elizabeth's praises. His eyes followed her as she proceeded from her mother to Bingley's best man, the one she had been laughing with so happily at the church. He wondered if another wedding was in the offing, and he tried to tear his gaze from her without success.

The meal was announced, and he offered his arm to Georgiana, who was looking oddly disappointed for some reason. In the dining room he was displeased to see that he was not seated with her, but a quick check of those who would be near her revealed no cause for concern, and he was, after all, a last-minute addition to the event. He could not help himself; as soon as Georgiana was seated, he began to scan the crowd for a sight of Elizabeth. She was not, as he had expected, with the wedding party; rather, she was seated slightly off to one side among people he did not know, her head slightly bowed in an uncharacteristic manner.

He walked around the table, looking for a card with his name. He experienced a sense of foreboding as he neared the place where Elizabeth sat, and was somehow unsurprised to discover that some mischievous fate had placed him beside her. He took a deep breath before seating himself.

Elizabeth, who had been awaiting his appearance, looked over at him. "We meet again, Mr. Darcy," she said, with a smile which would have been impish had she been more in spirits.

"So we do, Miss Bennet," he said evenly, thinking this was to be a very long meal indeed. To make matters worse, they were seated among a sea of Bingley's relatives who were unknown to him, making the prospect of other conversation poor as well. He smiled grimly, recalling dancing with her at the Netherfield ball and her challenge to him to converse with her. Well, he would show her that he had attended to her reproofs, no matter how painful it might be. "You seem to have made quite an impression on my sister," he said.

"It was unintentionally done," confessed Elizabeth, who had been wondering how to explain this very thing. "Miss Bingley introduced us, and I imagine she was feeling lonely." Realizing that this might sound like a criticism of his choice not to accompany Georgiana, she added quickly, "She is quite delightful, I must say. You must be very proud of her."

"Thank you," he said gravely. "I was surprised she wished to travel so far to attend Mr. Bingley's wedding, but she was quite insistent, even though there would be few people of her acquaintance here. She has, of course, known Mr. Bingley for a great many years, and looks to him almost as to another brother."

"I can sympathize with her; there are a great many more strangers here than I would have anticipated, but I gather Mr. Bingley has a very wide acquaintance."

"You seem to know his groomsman quite well." He had not meant his words to sound quite as accusing as they did, although it had been in his mind ever since he saw her walking down the aisle laughing with the man who had taken the place he had refused in the wedding. He had been indulging in the guilty pleasure of watching her during the wedding, storing up memories, and the sight of her clear enjoyment of another man's company had brought out an uncontrollable surge of bitterly painful jealousy. It had taken every ounce of self-control he possessed not to snatch her away at that moment.

She gave him a puzzled look. "Not well; we only met a few days ago. He is very amusing - he is to be married himself soon, and is already full of bridegroom's anxieties."

He felt a greater relief at her words than he would have thought possible. *What does it matter whether she looks at another man or not?* he chided himself. *She has made clear she wants nothing to do with you - what difference does it make who she chooses in your place?* Despite his efforts, though, he knew it did make a difference; it was hard enough knowing she would never be his, but the idea of her with another man was completely intolerable. *I should not have come,* he thought, not for the first time that day.

All subjects of conversation seemed to fail them at this point, and apart from the occasional half-hearted effort on each of their parts to comment on the food or the occasion, they remained mostly in a silence which grew increasingly painful to Elizabeth. She could not stop wondering what he was thinking of her; his countenance seemed to suggest that he was far from pleased with the current situation. She could not say why it was that she suddenly wished so fiercely to see the sort of smile she had sometimes seen on his face when he had looked at her in the past, or some sign of the man who had ended his letter with, "I will only add, God bless you."

She looked for comfort over towards Jane, and saw her blushing becomingly, her eyes cast down, as a smiling Bingley murmured something in her ear. The sense of pleasure she felt in this sight was tempered by the unexpected realization that she could no longer imagine herself ever being in Jane's place; at some point, having refused Mr. Darcy had transformed in her mind to a knowledge that she would not marry anyone else. A deep sense of loneliness filled her, and she looked down abruptly, wondering when it had happened that she had bound herself to him in such a manner. In the cold silence of the man at her side she heard an echo from the past: *I cannot forget the follies and vices of others so soon as I ought, nor their offenses against myself....My good opinion, once lost, is lost forever.* Little had she realized when she teased him that day how painfully this very characteristic would come to play against her.

It was more than she could bear. Fearing that her composure was at risk, Elizabeth hurriedly excused herself and slipped from the room. She sought out a back sitting room where she would be likely to be undisturbed, and took advantage of the quiet to try to calm her nerves. *It is not as serious as all that,* she lectured herself. *After all, nothing has actually changed; you are no worse off than you were last night. So you no longer have his good opinion - this cannot be of importance, given that you will be unlikely to see much of him in the future.* She would have to confide in Jane, she decided; if Jane knew the circumstances, she would help her avoid Mr. Darcy's company when he might visit Mr. Bingley. She could only wish that she found these plans to be reassuring instead of acutely painful.

She did not wish to face him again, and had the event been any other than Jane's wedding, nothing would have kept her from walking home to Longbourn at that moment, but she would do nothing to detract from Jane's memories of her special day. She decided simply to remain where she was until she was calm enough to face him once more. No one would trouble her there, and she could just curl up in the window seat and look outside.

She sat there for a brief period of time until she was startled by a noise from behind her. Embarrassed, she jumped to her feet from her inelegant position only to see Mr. Darcy standing just inside the doorway, his cheeks as flushed as hers.

"Pardon me, Miss Bennet," he said in a voice gentler than she had heard from him that day. "I did not wish to disturb you, only to tell you that I have decided to depart immediately, so you may return to the dining room whenever you wish. My regrets; it was never my intention to trouble you in any way." He bowed slightly, clearly preparing to leave.

"No, wait, please, Mr. Darcy," she said quickly. "Please do not leave on my account; I know how important your presence here today is to Mr. Bingley, whereas he may see me whenever he chooses. I will manage."

He shook his head. "I cannot allow that. I would not wish to make you uncomfortable, and I am the unexpected guest." His eyes were fixed upon her.

"Please, Mr. Darcy," she said in a low voice. "I will be far more uncomfortable if you leave early."

He looked at her, indecision clear in his expression. "If that is what you truly wish..."

"It is," she replied, aching from the tension in the air between them.

He did not look happy. "Well, then, I will leave when the other guests begin to depart, if that is agreeable to you."

"Thank you," she said.

"I shall trouble you no longer, then. Please allow me to apologize for disturbing you on a day which should have been joyful." He hesitated a moment before turning to depart.

Elizabeth felt a tight pain in her throat. "Only if you will accept my apologies as well for the untrue and unkind things I have said to you," she said.

Darcy was torn between a desire to leave and a wish to remain with her. "Miss Bennet, you are very kind, but I have long since acknowledged that the fault that evening was mine. It is not an occasion I look back upon with pride."

She had known that he must have regretted his choice to propose to her, but it was bitter to hear it so directly all the same; and she had trapped herself into a conversation which could have no happy resolution. She could think of nothing at all to say, and closed her eyes as she felt tears beginning to prick at them. "It is nothing, sir; please forget that I said anything," she said, and was horrified to hear her voice trembling. The pain in her chest only grew worse, and, realizing she could no longer control herself, she chose the incivility of turning her back on him over the humiliation of allowing him to see her cry. She could only hope that he would take her hint and leave her.

Her wish was not to be granted, however. Instead, she felt his hand touch her arm lightly. "Please, Miss Bennet," he said, his voice pained. "I am not worth your tears."

His words only heightened her own sense of loss and she began to cry harder, covering her face with her hands. He stood looking at her in indecision for a minute, feeling helpless in face of her pain which he could not explain; and then, with an exclamation, he gave in to instinct and put his arms around her in hope of comforting her.

She had no wish to fight him. Holding her handkerchief to her eyes, she rested her head upon his shoulder and wept uncontrollably. She knew only that his embrace offered her comfort and relief, and that she felt no desire to be anywhere else.

Darcy's heart ached for her pain, and he spoke words of consolation, urging her to calm herself; yet he found himself in the extraordinary position of both wanting to comfort her and hoping she remained in tears so he could hold her a little longer. This memory of having her in his arms would have to last him a lifetime, and he was not eager to let it go, especially after her free hand stole around his waist. He knew that she was not aware of what she was doing, but he allowed himself to imagine that she knew and was accepting him. "Please, Elizabeth, do not cry," he said, calling her by the name he always used in his thoughts, but had no right to speak. "It will not matter, it will be over soon." He only wished he understood her better, that he might have some clue as to why his appearance had upset her so deeply. "My sweet Elizabeth, I am so sorry; I never meant to hurt you," he said.

Gradually her storm of tears passed, and he waited for her to push him away, but instead she rested quietly in his embrace, making no move or protest. He tried to still his pounding heart, cautioning himself not to read anything into her choice when she was clearly still upset, but it was hard not to hope, and when hoping, to wish for more. He knew that he should release her and step away, but he could not bring himself to do so. Finally, when his conscience could no longer tolerate taking advantage of her distress, he said gently, "Miss Bennet?" She looked up at him from within his arms, her fine eyes still luminous with tears.

He could no more have kept from kissing her than he could have stopped the sun from rising in the east. Gently, tenderly, he brushed his lips against hers; and then, when she made no protest, he tasted the sweetness of her kiss again, allowing his lips to linger until he felt the intense pleasure of her own mouth pressing against his in a response that he had barely dared to dream of.

Elizabeth did not know what was the greatest surprise to her - that Mr. Darcy was kissing her, that she was allowing him to, or that the mere touch of his lips could give her such happiness. She wanted him never to stop, yet she knew they must stop, and that she should have stopped him long ago. *Just once more, and then I will stop,* she thought, and felt the pleasing rush of sensation as their lips met again. She knew if she kept looking at him she would be unable to resist the temptation he offered, so she laid her head on his shoulder once more. Her pulses fluttered as she thought of what had happened, and that she was finding happiness from being in his arms. She wished she could ask him whether he had meant the words he had said while she was crying, but she was afraid to speak. It was as if words might break the spell, or worse yet, lead to a resumption of the quarrelling, and that was a possibility she could not bear.

It seemed that he felt similarly since he was also silent, employing his time more gainfully by pressing slow, gentle kisses on her hair and forehead. It seemed far too short a time before he ceased his attentions for a few minutes and, with a formality that seemed foreign to the circumstances, said, "We have been away from the party far too long; people will be remarking on it, and it is not long before I must leave for London."

She could hear the remoteness in his voice, and it brought back in an instant the tightness in her chest. *He regrets this; he did not mean it to happen,* she thought. She could see all too easily how a man who had once had strong feelings for her would have been unable to resist the temptation she had offered, even if it went contrary to his current expectations and wishes. Well, she would not deny him his triumph; the tables had been well turned on her this time. Her pride, however, would not allow him to see how deeply she was wounded. She extracted herself from his embrace and stepped backwards, her chin held high. "I understand perfectly, Mr. Darcy," she said coolly.

He looked at her in puzzlement, but dared not ask what she meant. Instead he said only, "Shall I go back first, then?"

She inclined her head. "I think that would be best."

He could not understand her withdrawal - one moment she had been warmly compliant in his arms, and then the next as distant as the moon. Was she angry at him for his presumption? Anger did not seem to be in her mien, though. He resolved to move cautiously so as not to jeopardize their fragile understanding, and instead of the question he was longing to ask, he said humbly, "Miss Bennet, when I am able to come back to Netherfield, after Mr. and Mrs. Bingley return from their journey, would you permit me the honour of calling on you?"

The relief Elizabeth felt at his words was both extraordinary and transparent, as she realized that she had somehow misapprehended his previous expressions. For a moment she could not trust herself with words, but then she said, "I should like that very much, sir."

A rare smile grew slowly on his face, making him look quite appealing. He said softly, but with meaning, "Thank you."

Elizabeth could only watch as he turned to leave, feeling as if he was taking her heart with him. At the doorway, he paused and turned to look at her for a moment, then, without warning, he was at her side again, bending his head to kiss her once more. It was merely a light caress of his lips on hers, yet their mouths clung to each other. She was left gazing up at him longingly when he raised his head, and the look in his dark eyes assured her that he was no happier to stop than she.

Almost without thought he brushed her lips with his one last time. "I just wanted to be certain I had not dreamt it," he said softly.

"It would be a very sweet dream, then," replied Elizabeth with more of her usual vivacity than he had seen all day.

He touched her cheek lightly. "Very sweet indeed. I do not know what caused you to change your mind, but I am very glad you did. I will await you in the dining room....Elizabeth," he said, quietly invoking her name as if it were a privilege.

The intimacy of hearing him deliberately speak her name sent a shiver through her and she could only look at him, her heart in her eyes, as he left the room.

She sank into a chair, overwhelmed by the magnitude of what had passed between them. How could so much have changed so quickly? She had been so miserable, and now she was happy. She could not wait to tell Jane.

Her mouth twitched with amusement as she realized she had completely forgotten the greater change; that Jane was Mrs.

Bingley now, and Elizabeth would not be sharing this news with her that night as they prepared for bed. *No matter; it can wait,* she thought with a smile. What could not wait, she decided, was rejoining Mr. Darcy; if she had only a brief time with him before he was to depart, then she wished to make the most of it.

She stopped quickly in the dressing room to tidy herself. She splashed cool water on her face until she could no longer see traces of tears when she looked in the small mirror, but nothing would disguise the heightened color in her lips and cheeks. She pressed her hands to her face, remembering his kisses. Nothing would ever be the same again.

Finding her way back to the dining room, she felt a moment's hesitation when she entered; a sense of disorientation, as if somehow once she saw him again, he would again be the hostile stranger from the church. But as she came up to him, he turned a look of such pleasure on her that she could think of nothing else.

"Miss Bennet, I hope you are feeling better," he said with a suppressed smile.

Elizabeth saw their neighbours' eyes turned on her. "Ah... yes, thank you; it was merely a touch of headache. A little fresh air was all I needed," she said.

His eyes caressed her. "I am glad to hear it."

She coloured; and in her embarrassment she felt somewhat lost for words, until she recalled his earlier comment wondering what had changed her mind. She turned a lively look on him, and said, "Mr. Darcy, I do not believe that I mentioned to you I had the opportunity to travel to Derbyshire earlier this summer."

"Did you, Miss Bennet?" Darcy's tone was rather more suited for lovemaking than casual conversation, and Elizabeth swallowed hard.

"Yes, I was touring with my aunt and uncle, and we saw many of the sights - the Peaks, Chatsworth, Dove Dale - it is a lovely region, I must say. I even had the opportunity, at my aunt's insistence, to tour Pemberley."

His eyebrows shot upward with surprise. "*You* were at *Pemberley?*"

"Yes, quite a coincidence, is it not?"

"Yes, it is," he said slowly, as if uncertain what to make of this intelligence. "And did you enjoy your tour?"

"Oh, very much. The house is delightful and the grounds are quite charming," she said, her eyes sparkling with mischief. "I must admit, though, that my *favourite* part was talking to your housekeeper, Mrs. Reynolds."

He looked somewhat dubious. "Though I am very fond of Mrs. Reynolds, and she is a valued member of my household, I find it rather surprising that you would find *her* the most interesting part of Pemberley."

"Perhaps it was because I found her conversation very enlightening, especially on the subject of the family," said Elizabeth. Dropping her voice, she added, "She gave you what my aunt called a most flaming character. She gave *me* a great deal to think about."

Understanding dawned in his eyes, and he smiled slightly. "I clearly should recompense Mrs. Reynolds better for her services," he said. He sought out her hand under the table with his and clasped it tightly.

Elizabeth was rather startled, but not displeased, to find the sober Mr. Darcy to have an element of the playful and not quite proper schoolboy about him. He moved the conversation to obtaining her opinion of the more usual attractions of Pemberley, but as he did so, he caressed the back of her hand with his thumb in a manner which she found unexpectedly distracting.

When the meal drew to a close not long after, Darcy, although maintaining every evidence of propriety, made no effort to disguise his intention to monopolize her company until his departure. He was surprised that Georgiana did not attempt to join them immediately; she clearly was making great strides in conquering her shyness. But all too soon it was time for him to make his departure. He convinced Elizabeth to accompany him as he bid his farewells to Mr. and Mrs. Bingley.

As soon as they reached them, Bingley looked at Darcy so expressively and shook hands with him with such a warmth as left no doubt of his observation of the change between them, a fact which made Elizabeth colour and Darcy to look at him with the lively suspicion that only one who had moved so recently as he from a state of desolation to one of elation could manage. If Jane had noted any difference, she was more subtle in her reaction than her new husband, to the relief of Elizabeth, who was not yet prepared to reveal to the world in general, and her mother in particular, Mr. Darcy's intentions.

She found herself accompanying him out to his carriage. Georgiana, who had decided to ride back to London with her brother instead of with the couple who had previously arranged to take her, stood nearby, suddenly fascinated by the trees in front of Netherfield as her brother took Elizabeth's hand and kissed it lightly. He managed to caress her fingers as he released them, and Elizabeth shivered.

"I hope we shall meet again soon, Miss Bennet," he said, his voice tender.

"I shall look forward to it, sir," she replied with the lively smile which had first attracted him to her all those months ago.

"Georgiana," Darcy said, his eyes still lingering on Elizabeth, "it is time for us to depart."

Georgiana turned, and to the surprise of all, threw her arms around Elizabeth in a warm embrace. She had watched them closely earlier, noticing first their sobriety, then their joint absence, and her brother's obvious happiness after his return. She had been relieved beyond measure to see his smile again, and amused by the realization that he was holding Miss Bennet's hand under the table.

Over Miss Darcy's shoulder, Elizabeth's startled eyes met her brother's. Georgiana whispered, "Thank you," then allowed Darcy to hand her into the carriage. With one last, serious look at Elizabeth, Darcy entered the carriage as well. As it drove off, Elizabeth stood and watched until it had disappeared from sight.

With the evidence no longer before her, she began to feel a certain confused disbelief - could it truly be that Mr. Darcy had held her in his arms, had *kissed* her. She hugged herself for a moment, then silently turned back to the house.

No sooner had she put in an appearance than Jane sought her out and drew her aside. "Dearest Lizzy, I must know - what has happened?" she said quietly.

Elizabeth's eyes danced mischievously. "What has happened?" she teased. "You have married Mr. Bingley - that is what has happened!"

"Oh, please, be serious, Lizzy - with Mr. Darcy, of course! You cannot be so cruel as to let me go away for so long without knowing," she said persuasively.

"And I am sure Mr. Bingley is waiting eagerly to hear this as well!"

Jane coloured. "Well, he *is* very concerned - he has been so worried about Mr. Darcy, and then he arranged to seat you together, hoping you would have the opportunity to work out your differences."

*So it had not been a coincidence,* thought Elizabeth with some amusement. "Well, then, you may tell him that his plan succeeded, and Mr. Darcy now has a good understanding of how my views of him have altered. He asked to call on me once you and Bingley have returned."

Her eyes lit up. "He did?" she exclaimed excitedly. "What did you say, Lizzy?"

Elizabeth was quite tempted to tease, but she could see how much this meant to Jane. "I told him I would like that," she said warmly.

Jane threw her arms around Elizabeth. "Oh, I am so happy! This is the best gift I could have received today."

"Yes, and you have a new husband who thinks *you* are the best gift he has ever received, and you should return to him," Elizabeth said lightly. "I will write you a letter and tell you everything, I promise." *Well, there might be a few details I shall leave out,* she thought with good humour, recalling the feeling of his arms around her and the exquisite sensation of his kiss.

Elizabeth thought over her meeting with Darcy frequently in the next days, trying to recall each word and intimation, often with pleasure, but sometimes with anxiety when she thought of how long it would be until she saw him again. It would be a full two months before the Bingleys returned to Netherfield, and a great deal could happen in that time - including a change of heart towards a woman who, on reflection, had given him far more pain than pleasure. To make matters worse, she had no way to know whether his feelings had changed, since there could be no contact between them. She even half-hoped that Miss Darcy might think to write, just for news of his existence, but she knew that their acquaintance was far too slight to warrant such correspondence; so she resigned herself as best as she could to waiting.

She had decided not to tell her family about Mr. Darcy's interest in her until she was certain he intended to return - which would, unfortunately, likely not be until she learned of his return to Netherfield, if it did indeed occur. She did not want to face the foolishness of disappointed hopes in public, and she knew without the shadow of a doubt that her mother could not possibly keep such news to herself.

Mr. Darcy had been quite clear she was not to expect him before the Bingleys' return to Netherfield, so it was with no little surprise that only two weeks later she heard Kitty announce the news that he was riding up the lane. She coloured; surely this must mean that his intentions were unchanged, but why would he be returning so early? More importantly, how was she to explain it to her family? She quickly turned her mind to the question of how to most quickly extricate him from the bosom of her family, but had only a moment before his knock at the door.

She waited anxiously for him to be announced, but as she watched the door, she saw Hill leading him past the sitting room. He glanced in for only a moment as he passed, just managing to catch Elizabeth's eye; his expression was serious, almost grave, as she had known it to be in the past. Her pulses fluttered as she realized where he must be going, and an even deeper flush stole up her cheeks at not only the idea of him speaking to her father, but how her father was likely to receive him.

"Lord, I wonder what *he* is doing here?" asked Lydia.

"No doubt he is passing through, and has a letter or some intelligence of Mrs. Bingley," Mrs. Bennet replied. "Well, any friend of Mr. Bingley's will always be welcome here; but else I must say that I hate the very sight of him. Why, he is too proud to even stop to pay his compliments to us!" Mrs. Bennet's delight in pronouncing Jane's new name was undiminished in two weeks of practice. Kitty and Lydia looked at one another and giggled.

*This is a poor beginning indeed!* thought Elizabeth.

"I believe he is here to see me," she said evenly.

"What nonsense you talk, Lizzy! Why would he come to see *you?* We all know what he thinks of you!" cried Mrs. Bennet.

Elizabeth shrugged lightly, for all the world as if she did not know the explosion which was to follow her words. "Perhaps, but he did ask at Jane's wedding for my permission to call on me; and I gave it."

The effect of her words was most extraordinary; for on hearing them, Mrs. Bennet sat quite still, and unable to utter a syllable. She was not in general backward to credit what was for the advantage of her family, or that came in the shape of a lover to any of them, but it was many minutes while Elizabeth waited in agony for Darcy's appearance until she could comprehend it.

Her sisters were not so slow. "Not Mr. Darcy!" cried Lydia. "Lizzy, you must be joking! Lord, he is *so* dull, and we all know of the infamous way he treated dear Mr. Wickham!"

"He is too proud to speak to the likes of us!" added Kitty, laughing at the very idea.

Elizabeth could only hope that their manners would be improved by the time Mr. Darcy was done with her father. She kept a closer eye on her mother, who was still fanning herself and gazing at Elizabeth in shock. She had certainly hoped to have more time than this to acquaint her family with the idea.

Finally the dam broke on Mrs. Bennet's words. "Good gracious! Lord bless me! only think! dear me! oh, Lizzy, why did you say *nothing*? Your hair, your gown... but it is too late, we can only hope - Oh! my sweetest Lizzy! I am so pleased - so happy."

She clearly would have continued for some time in this vein, had not Elizabeth interrupted to say, "He asked only to *call*, no more; and he will no doubt be here any minute. Please, can we speak of something else?"

"Oh, Lord!" cried her mother, fidgeting about in her chair. "Of course he will be here. Mary, Kitty, Lydia - you must go upstairs - no, you must go to Meryton! Yes, Meryton will do - and my dear, dear Lizzy!" She came to Elizabeth and pinched her cheeks to bring colour to them, hardly a necessary task at the moment, and to smooth her hair. "Oh, it will have to do, but why did you not warn me, Lizzy? Such a charming man! So handsome, so tall!"

"There is no account for sending my sisters away," objected Elizabeth, who could not help being amused as she recalled the same ploy being used on Jane.

"Oh, there most certainly is!" Mrs. Bennet waved her hands at the younger girls, urging them on to a hasty departure.

Elizabeth could only imagine with embarrassment what Mr. Darcy would make of this scene. She hoped desperately that her mother's effusions would be over by the time he came, though she was also beginning to worry about what might be keeping Mr. Darcy so long with her father. And the implications of what it meant that he was talking to her father was not something she was ready to consider.

At that moment the two gentlemen appeared. Elizabeth's eyes flew immediately to Darcy, and she was a little relieved by his smile. Not even her worries about her parents' want of propriety could stop the burst of pleasure she felt on seeing him, and he seemed reassured by her appearance as well.

Her father sent her an amused look, and said dryly, "Well, Lizzy, it seems that Mr. Darcy has ridden all the way from London today to see you." He clearly anticipated that this would come as quite a shock to her.

"I hope it was a pleasant ride, sir," she said calmly. "Would you care to sit?"

Mr. Bennet, taken aback, quickly excused himself as Darcy paid his respects to Mrs. Bennet and then to Elizabeth.

It was an uncomfortable moment; Elizabeth had never considered what she might say in these circumstances. She asked after his sister, who he reassured her was in excellent health, and about his stay in town. To Elizabeth's great relief, her mother luckily stood in such awe of their guest that she ventured not to speak to him, unless it was in her power to offer him any attention, or mark her deference for his opinion. This formal conversation continued for some time, with too much discomfort on the part of the main participants to do more than allow their eyes to meet on occasion, until Mrs. Bennet remembered that she was wanted elsewhere. Elizabeth rolled her eyes at the blatancy of this maneuver, but knew there was no use in protest.

Once they were alone, Darcy looked at her with great warmth. "Elizabeth," he said, his voice replete with feeling. She coloured, and dropped her eyes in embarrassment, a pointless effort since he took advantage of the moment to take her hand in his and raise it to his lips. The sensation produced by his kiss seemed to race down her arm like electricity, leaving her momentarily speechless. He asked tentatively, "You have not changed your mind?"

She responded to him with an arch smile. "Not in the last weeks; although we both have reason to know, sir, that my opinions are not entirely unalterable, I do not intend to change them again. But *you* are before your time, Mr. Darcy."

His smile slowly grew at her teasing. "Before I respond to that, let me ask you this: how long do we have before your mother returns?" He had not relinquished her hand, a state of affairs which she was finding surprisingly distracting.

Elizabeth felt a lurch inside at his words. "We have all the time in the world - were it within my mother's power, I am sure she would post armed guards at the door to make sure we are not disturbed." She glanced at him quickly to see how he took this additional evidence of impropriety on her family's part, but he seemed not in the least displeased.

"You should, perhaps, not have told me that," he said, but his tone implied quite the opposite. "But I will take the time to answer your question then - I came early because I wanted to see you. I realized that the only reason to delay was so that I could court you without bringing it to public notice, and I decided to risk the possible embarrassment of having you refuse me publicly if it meant I did not need to wait out two very long months."

"And you decided to begin with my father?" she asked mischievously.

He looked slightly embarrassed. "I thought that if I was to be open about this, I might as well do it properly; so I asked his permission to call on you. He seemed ... quite stunned."

She coloured at the implied question. "I thought it best not to mention the possibility, in case you were to change your mind."

"I, change my mind?" he said in a surprised voice. "I cannot imagine why you would think that."

She looked down. "What may occur in the heat of the moment may not always be what might be wished for in a moment of more sober reflection."

This comment was met by silence. Finally, in a carefully neutral voice, Darcy said, "What is it that you have wished for in your moments of sober reflection?"

She gave him a sidelong glance with a smile. "Surely, Mr. Darcy, you cannot expect me to answer that question!"

"You have not regretted it?"

With a teasing look, she said, "No, I have not; but I believe I have already told you that, sir."

His relief was so great that he acted without thought, catching her face in his hand and caressing her lips with his for a mere moment. "Then do not say such things!" He had clearly startled her with his behaviour, and he cursed himself and his lack of self-control.

Elizabeth was experiencing the shock of sensation that came with his touch. It had been all too brief, yet she knew she should not have allowed it in the first place. "What should I say, then?" she asked archly.

Darcy drew in a quick breath. Was she *flirting* with him? If so, he would need to be very careful indeed; he was by no means certain of his self-control when she looked at him like that. Choosing his words with care, he said, "While there are a great number of things I should *like* to hear you say, I think that we both know what you *should* say, and it involves reproaching me for my behaviour."

She smiled as if at some inner joke. "I cannot disagree, though I would have to admit that I am a few weeks late in saying it."

He was beginning to see that there were flaws in his earlier reasoning that a gradual wooing, giving her time to truly get to know him, was the best option. "Be careful, Elizabeth," he said softly. "You do not know how you tempt me."

Elizabeth had a strong impulse to ask him to tell her just how she did tempt him, but she checked herself, reminding herself of how her liveliness had led her astray with him in the past. She wished she knew what was in his mind; he evidently did not intend to propose to her yet, though he must know from her behaviour that she would not refuse - could not, after allowing him to kiss her, not just once, but several times without protest. Perhaps he was not as certain of his choice as he appeared. He had spoken of the possibility of his embarrassment if she refused him - but was there anything to stop him from changing his mind, leaving her to face the humiliation of being jilted? The very thought was painful enough; she resolved to be less forward, and to remember that he had by no means made a commitment.

Darcy saw her smile fade somewhat, and berated himself anew, realizing that once again he had gone too far. He reminded himself yet again that the behaviour she had permitted during a moment of distress was likely to be unacceptable in a calmer frame of mind. Unfortunately, his desperate desire to taste her lips again was such as to keep countering his rational mind, and that slight contact had not been enough to do more than to whet his need for her.

He was a man torn; he wanted a return of her teasing smiles and flirtatious looks, but he knew how very effectively they would undermine his restraint. "Eliz....Miss Bennet," he said, "I must throw myself on your mercy. I want.... I would *like* to give you time to come to know me. My ability to be patient, however, is not what it ought to be where you are concerned; and most especially when you are... welcoming to me. You do not know the effect you have on me. Please understand if I need to keep a certain distance in order to maintain a standard of behaviour."

A sense of relief filled Elizabeth at his words. "I do not object," she said gently, "if you wish to call me by my name when we are alone."

He expelled his breath slowly. Any other woman he would have assumed to have misunderstood him, but this was Elizabeth - had she failed to take his meaning, or was she challenging him? "You are very kind."

Elizabeth looked at him sympathetically. She knew how difficult it would have been for her to restrain her happiness at seeing him, and he had waited longer for her and had more reason to be uncertain of his reception at her hands. He was once again reassuring her of his intentions, yet he had clearly decided not to take advantage of her earlier permissive behaviour to stake a claim to her, as he could have so easily - she could not have denied that she had allowed him to take liberties with her. "It seems rather too late," she said carefully, "for me to be *Missish*, and I would prefer not to try." She could hardly be more obvious than that, and she waited anxiously to see his reaction.

It seemed an unconscionably long time before he took her words in, and even then he appeared not to quite credit them. "I do not want to rush you," he said uncertainly.

She considered telling him directly that he was not rushing her, but decided she could not be so impossibly forward, even given his obvious provocation. She limited herself to giving him an eloquent look in flagrant disregard of his request for distance.

His face remained unreadable for a moment, then she discovered a new light in his eyes, one which made her tremble. His hand reached up and caressed her cheek, then brushed across her neck to finally cradle her chin. "Elizabeth," he said, his voice slightly unsteady, "This would be a good time to tell me to stop."

She gave him a mischievous look. "I have taken your opinion into account, sir."

A trace of a smile crossed his face. He leaned toward her slowly until his lips caressed hers lightly. The experience was every bit as pleasurable as he recalled. "My sweetest, loveliest Elizabeth," he whispered before kissing her once again.

If Elizabeth had thought the experience of his kiss was powerful when she was despairing, it was nothing to the shivering tendrils of desire that it sent through her now, when their understanding was quite different. The feelings were new to her, and rather startling in their intensity; but she trusted Darcy, and would not let her own reaction frighten her.

Darcy, feeling his control beginning to slip, drew back slightly, gazing with great pleasure into her lovely eyes. Her kisses had been both very exciting and remarkably sweet, and had only increased his longing to ask even more of her, but he knew she had already been unreasonably generous with him. He did not think he could stop himself from kissing her again - no, the truth was that he felt absolutely no desire to stop himself, no matter how much he reminded himself of the dangers inherent in such behaviour. "Perhaps if you do not think it a good time to tell me to stop, you might consider it a good time to tell me that you will be my wife," he said.

His words astonished him; until he began to speak, he had no intention of proposing to her again so quickly, but it seemed his desire for her was to be expressed one way or another. He awaited her response with an anxious agony, ready to withdraw his words at her slightest evidence of discomfort.

Her eyes danced. "Very well, if you insist, sir," she said; then, quickly recognizing this was not a teasing matter for him, she added, "I should be quite happy to agree to *that* suggestion."

It was more than he could believe. How could it be so simple, after all this time and suffering? -- that she should simply agree? Her look told him it was true, and a slow smile began to grow on his face. "It seems, then, that I am destined to spend a great deal of my visit today speaking to your father," he said, his voice low, "so I had best make good use of the time I have with you."

To his delight, she met him halfway this time as he kissed her. He was intoxicated with the thought that she would be his, that she would be with him every day, and that there would come to be a time when he would not have to restrain his desire for her. He poured that exhilaration into his kiss, claiming an equal response from her. Knowing how easily he could lose himself in her, he forced himself to stop long before he was ready, but was rewarded by the entrancing sight of Elizabeth with her lovely eyes dark with passion for him.

"My beloved Elizabeth," he said, "how I wish I could take you away with me today!"

She gave him a look of mock demureness. "I do not imagine my father would be pleased with *that* idea!"

He smiled at her teasing, but his countenance turned quickly serious again. "And you? Would it please you?"

She regarded him for a moment, struck by his apparent need for reassurance as to her feelings for him. She felt a lurch of sadness at the thought of all the pain he had suffered on her account, that he should doubt her affection when she had made it so plain. *Well, in this matter, he can have all the reassurance he needs!* she thought with pleased determination. "My dearest," she said warmly, "I can think of nothing I would like more than to be with you." With great daring, she reached up to kiss him lightly, but what began as a simple gesture of affection quickly turned into more as they sought to express all that they felt in a manner which could not be misunderstood.

Some weeks later, Elizabeth joined Darcy and Georgiana at Netherfield as they awaited the return of the Bingleys from their tour. Elizabeth was anxious to see Jane; there was so much she wished to tell her, and to hear from her. She glanced at Darcy affectionately, and saw her smile provoked that smoldering look which told her that, but for the presence of his sister, he would be expressing himself in a manner more suited to a man violently in love. *It is astonishing*, she thought, not for the first time, *that a mere look from him is enough to set my heart racing!*

It had not always been an easy journey to this point. Mr. Bennet had expressed some strong reservations about a match made so suddenly, and with a man of whom he had heard so many ill reports; but with time, as he saw more of Darcy with Elizabeth and grew to know him better, he became convinced of the value of his future son-in-law. The two lovers also had their share of painful discussions as they worked to resolve their past misunderstandings and to grow to a greater knowledge of one another. There had been far more times of happiness than of trouble, though, and the delight of Georgiana in their engagement was beyond her ability to express.

The carriage arrived, and a flurry of happy embraces and congratulations which could finally be made in person ensued. Elizabeth had never seen Jane happier, and the bond between her and Mr. Bingley was almost palpable. They talked about their tour and their visit to Mr. Bingley's relatives excitedly, and Elizabeth shared all the news from Longbourn and Meryton. Darcy was mostly quiet, but an occasional glance at him showed Elizabeth that it was a silence of contentment rather than of distress.

Georgiana, shy as ever, quickly excused herself from the scene of the reunion, and it was not long afterwards that Bingley announced that it was time for them to refresh themselves from the effects of a long day's travel. There was something in the way his eyes rested on Jane, however, that led Elizabeth, with her now greater knowledge of these matters, to believe that it might be some time before the couple made a reappearance. She smiled at the warm look in Jane's eyes as she blushed lightly before withdrawing, and watched after the disappearing couple with deep satisfaction over their apparent felicity.

She was not the only one with such thoughts, she discovered, as she felt a pair of warm arms slip around her from behind. She rested back against his beloved form, trembling at the rush of desire that ran through her as his lips delicately explored the sensitive skin of her neck. It was a familiar feeling now, that aching need that he could provoke in her so easily, especially as his proficiency in delighting her senses grew. She bore the subtle torture of his touch as long as she could, then turned to catch his mouth with hers, no longer afraid or ashamed to show him her desire. After sating herself with the pleasure of his lips, she leaned against him once more with a contented sigh.

"Soon, my dearest," he whispered in her ear. "Soon it will be our turn."

# Such Differing Reports

*I've always felt that Charlotte Lucas was underrated. She may have married a foolish man, but her observations were always spot on. Elizabeth should have known that, yet she ignores Charlotte more than once when her friend suggests that Mr. Darcy is partial to her. What would have happened if Elizabeth had believed her?*

DARCY FELT THE NOW-FAMILIAR pounding of his heart as he approached the parsonage at Hunsford. The prospect of being in the same room with Miss Elizabeth Bennet, of seeing the sparkle in her fine eyes, of breathing the very air she breathed, was enough to make him dizzy. He should be avoiding her. His fascination with her was placing him at risk of exciting her expectations. Darcy shook his head in disgust. Who was he trying to fool? He was the moth to her flame, and he could not stay away. At least Mrs. Collins and her sister would be there to protect him from saying anything foolish.

The maid let him in, bobbing a clumsy curtsey. He strode past her to the drawing room and opened the door to see Elizabeth leaning down to slide a letter into the drawer of the small writing desk. Her face held a startled expression, like that of a doe in the woods. The sunlight pouring in the window behind her made her simple blue dress appear to shimmer around the edges. Darcy was so dazzled that it was a moment before he realized she was alone.

Why had the maid said nothing? But he could not bring himself to regret the opportunity to have Elizabeth to himself.

Belatedly he bowed. "I apologize for my intrusion, Miss Bennet. I had understood all the ladies to be within."

She gave him an arch look as she pushed the drawer closed behind her. "Mrs. Collins and Miss Lucas are gone on business into the village. They should not be away long."

He took the seat she indicated, responding automatically to her enquiries after Rosings, more interested in her lively expression than in her words. As usual, he hardly knew what to say in her presence, but it was enough to look upon her.

After a few moments of silence, she said, "How very suddenly you all quitted Netherfield last November, Mr. Darcy! It must have been a most agreeable surprise to Mr. Bingley to see you all after him so soon; for, if I recollect right, he went but the day before. He and his sisters were well, I hope, when you left London."

"Perfectly so—I thank you."

There was another short pause before she replied, "I think I have understood that Mr. Bingley has not much idea of ever returning to Netherfield again?"

He was impressed by her calm words. No other lady would have shown such an understanding of his need to protect his friend, when it involved denying her sister an advantageous marriage. But perhaps Elizabeth saw no need for her sister to marry well because she pictured herself as the future mistress of Pemberley. He must be more careful to hide his feelings. "I have never heard him say so; but it is probable that he may spend very little of his time there in future. He has many friends, and he is at a time of life when friends and engagements are continually increasing."

"If he means to be but little at Netherfield, it would be better for the neighbourhood that he should give up the place entirely, for then we might possibly get a settled family there. But perhaps Mr. Bingley did not take the house so much for the convenience of the neighbourhood as for his own, and we must expect him to keep or quit it on the same principle."

"I should not be surprised," said Darcy, "if he were to give it up, as soon as any eligible purchase offers."

Elizabeth made no answer, turning her face from him. Did she know that her profile fascinated him? If only he could taste her delicate cheekbones with his lips. In an attempt to steer his mind away from that delightful prospect, he said, "This seems a very comfortable house. Lady Catherine, I believe, did a great deal to it when Mr. Collins first came to Hunsford." It was a reminder of the difference in their station.

"I believe she did—and I am sure she could not have bestowed her kindness on a more grateful object." Elizabeth gave him an arch look.

He smiled at her graceful acknowledgment of her cousin's flaws. "Mr. Collins appears very fortunate in his choice of a wife."

"Yes, indeed; his friends may well rejoice in his having met with one of the very few sensible women who would have accepted him, or have made him happy if they had. My friend has an excellent understanding—though I am not certain that I consider her marrying Mr. Collins as the wisest thing she ever did. She seems perfectly happy, however, and in a prudential light, it is certainly a very good match for her."

Was she giving him a hint? He cast about for words. "It must be very agreeable to her to be settled within so easy a distance of her own family and friends."

"An easy distance do you call it? It is nearly fifty miles."

"And what is fifty miles of good road? Little more than half a day's journey. Yes, I call it a very easy distance."

"I should never have considered the distance as one of the advantages of the match," cried Elizabeth. "I should never have said Mrs. Collins was settled near her family."

Her vehemence caught him by surprise until he

remembered her propensity for stating opinions not her own. He was quite willing to tease back. "It is a proof of your own attachment to Hertfordshire. Any thing beyond the very neighbourhood of Longbourn, I suppose, would appear far."

A pretty flush crept up Elizabeth's cheeks. "I do not mean to say that a woman may not be settled too near her family. The far and the near must be relative, and depend on many varying circumstances. Where there is fortune to make the expense of travelling unimportant, distance becomes no evil. But that is not the case here. Mr. and Mrs. Collins have a comfortable income, but not such a one as will allow of frequent journeys—and I am persuaded my friend would not call herself near her family under less than half the present distance."

He could not help himself. He drew his chair a little towards her, and said, "You cannot have a right to such very strong local attachment. You cannot have been always at Longbourn." The intoxicating scent of Elizabeth and rosewater drifted over him.

Elizabeth looked surprised, and he realized he had gone too far. He drew back his chair, took a newspaper from the table, and glanced over it. When he thought he could trust his voice, he asked, "Are you pleased with Kent?"

A short dialogue on the subject of the country ensued, on either side calm and concise—and soon put an end to by the entrance of Mrs. Collins and her sister, just returned from their walk. Mrs. Collins' look of surprise at their tête-à-tête reminded Darcy of the impropriety of his visit, and he related the mistake which had occasioned his intruding on Miss Bennet. He hardly knew what else to say, and made his excuses to depart as soon as he could.

Still, his feet seemed to drag as he set off down the path to Rosings. He wanted to see Elizabeth's arch smile again, but he could see clearly that he was in more danger than he thought. He would have to stay away from the parsonage. But even as he thought it, he knew that by the next morning, his resolve would have paled before his need to be in her presence.

"What can be the meaning of this!" said Charlotte, as soon as he was gone. "My dear Eliza, he must be in love with you, or he would never have called on us in this familiar way."

"I can hardly think so, Charlotte," Elizabeth reassured her with a laugh. "You were not here; we could hardly keep a conversation going! Each time I raised a subject, he would exhaust it in a few words, and then lapse into silence. He is so far from being in love with me as to be loathe even to converse with me!"

"I suppose it is not very likely, then," agreed her friend, "yet he does appear to have quite an interest in you. Have you never noticed how he watches you? – and you were the only lady apart from Bingley's sisters he honoured with his hand for a dance at the Netherfield ball."

Elizabeth put a hand affectionately on Charlotte's shoulder. "He looks at me only to criticize, dearest Charlotte! Do you not recall that he found me tolerable, but not handsome enough to tempt him?" She imitated his voice as she repeated his words with a smile.

Charlotte continued to look dubious, however. "We shall see, I suppose. But Eliza, just think – if you were to have made such a conquest!" There was not a doubt in her mind that all her friend's dislike would vanish, if she could suppose him to be in her power. But she did not think it right to press the subject any further, from the danger of raising expectations which might only end in disappointment.

Afterwards Elizabeth found that she could not put the conversation out of her mind. Mr. Darcy in love with her? It seemed a completely ridiculous notion, yet Charlotte's judgment and observation in these matters had often proved better than her own. She could not believe it to be true, but she found that she could not completely discount the idea either, and resolved to observe him more closely in the future

She had ample opportunity, as the two cousins found a temptation from this period of walking to the Parsonage almost every day. They called at various times of the morning, sometimes separately, sometimes together, and now and then accompanied by their aunt. It was plain to Elizabeth that Colonel Fitzwilliam came because he had pleasure in their society, a persuasion which of course recommended him still more; and she was reminded by her own satisfaction in being with him, as well as by his evident admiration, of her former favourite George Wickham; and though, in comparing them, she saw there was less captivating softness in Colonel Fitzwilliam's manners, she believed he might have the best informed mind.

But why Mr. Darcy came so often to the Parsonage, it was very difficult to understand. With Charlotte's caution in mind, Elizabeth watched him covertly when they next were at Rosings; but without much success. She knew not what to make of him. He certainly looked at her a great deal, but the expression of that look was disputable. It was an earnest, steadfast gaze, but she doubted whether there were much admiration in it, and sometimes it seemed nothing but absence of mind.

No sooner would she reach the resolution that her initial impression of him had been correct than sudden doubts would assail her. On his visits to Hunsford he frequently sat there ten minutes together without opening his lips; and when he did speak, it seemed the effect of necessity rather than of choice – a sacrifice to propriety, not a pleasure to himself. He seldom appeared really animated, and this seemed absolute proof of his disinterest, but then Colonel Fitzwilliam's occasionally laughing at his stupidity, proved that he was generally different. Her own knowledge of him could not have told her that, and she began to wonder why he was so different in her company.

She did not begin to be concerned that his feelings were seriously engaged, however, until once in her ramble within the Park she unexpectedly met him. She assumed that he would meet her with a few formal enquiries and an awkward pause and then away, but to her surprise he actually thought it necessary to turn back and walk with her. He did not say a great deal, nor did she give herself the trouble of talking much, but he seemed to attend to her more intimately than was strictly necessary, and there was that in his manner which seemed somehow different from his behaviour in her presence in the past. She could not quite identify what the difference was, but afterwards, as she thought back upon the occasion, she decided that it would be best not to offer him anything which might be seen as encouragement.

She was sensible to the compliment of such a man's affection, though she could not help but be bewildered by how it had come to pass that he should admire her, after having withstood her charms at their earlier meetings. Apart from his request to dance with her at Netherfield, there had been nothing resembling a courtship. She supposed it must be a passing fancy, since so proud a man would certainly never propose to a woman with her low connections. Still, she did not desire to occasion any pain to him, and so determined to do her best to put a stop to any ideas he might have about her interest in him.

Therefore she was prepared the following day when once again she came upon him in the grove. His presence there was confirmation enough of her suspicions, as there would be no reason for him to be in that same spot unless he was awaiting her. He again said little, but at one point seemed to suggest that on her future visits to Kent she would be staying at Rosings. Startled, she realized this was more serious than she had thought.

She chose her words with care. "Mr. Darcy," she said

slowly, "I wonder if I might ask your opinion on something."

He placed his hand over her gloved one. "Certainly. I would be happy to be of use to you."

She could feel the warmth of his hand through her glove. This was not proceeding as she had planned. "Suppose, sir, you had a sister whom you loved dearly."

He looked at her in surprise. "That is not at all difficult to imagine, since I do have a such a sister."

Emboldened, Elizabeth continued. "Suppose, then, that she met a gentleman who engaged her affections, and who appeared to return them. But then he disappeared without word, leaving everyone to suppose his friends had interfered with the match. Would you be inclined to think kindly toward those friends?"

His brow darkened, and Elizabeth feared she had gone too far in her accusation. But she would not allow his anger to intimidate her, so she stood her ground.

He spoke finally through clenched teeth, saying each word distinctly. "What did he tell you?"

Elizabeth shook her head in confusion. "He? The gentleman, or his friend?"

"You know perfectly well of whom I speak. I repeat, what did he tell you?"

"Indeed, sir, neither of them told me anything. It was merely an observation...."

"I must know. What did Wickham tell you?"

Elizabeth blinked. "Mr. Wickham? What has he to do with this?"

"Everything, as you well know! What did he say about my sister?"

She was beginning to feel frightened by his anger, and took a step away. "*Your* sister, sir? Why, nothing to speak of."

She could see he was trying to calm himself. "Miss Bennet,

I must insist you tell me. It is a matter of the utmost urgency."

For a moment she almost took pity on his clear distress, but the illogical nature of the conversation stopped those natural feelings. "He spoke very little of her, only to say she was handsome and highly accomplished."

"But what of his connection to her?"

"Why, nothing, except that she had been fond of him when she was a child, before she became proud like...." She realized just in time the danger of what she was about to say.

His mouth curled. "As a child, indeed. Why, then, did you raise this question to me, if he said nothing more to you?"

"This question? What question?"

"About my sister!"

Finally, comprehension dawned, though the matter of Mr. Wickham's connection remained a mystery. "I was speaking of my own sister, Mr. Darcy, not yours."

"*Your* sister?"

"Yes, my dear Jane, who is now not only heart-broken but also exposed to the world's derision for disappointed hopes!" The thought of Jane's distress renewed Elizabeth's anger toward Mr. Darcy. "And if I am not mistaken, you were pleased by the outcome!"

His countenance changed as if she had slapped him. "I cannot deny it."

His proud words removed the last vestiges of control from her temper. "I believe I have heard quite enough. Good day, Mr. Darcy." She turned her back on him in what she hoped was an unmistakeable manner, then walked off without a backwards look. The nerve of the man, to admit straight out that he had opposed a match between Mr. Bingley and Jane! At least he could no longer be in doubt as to her own feelings toward him. She doubted he would trouble her again.

Darcy could not take his eyes from Elizabeth's light figure

until she vanished into the trees, but the disturbance of his mind took away his usual pleasure at the sight. How had their conversation gone awry so quickly? One moment he had been warmed with pleasure at the idea that she was seeking his advice, then a moment later …. He did not even wish to think of it.

Wickham. The cur had a malevolent talent for ruining happy moments in Darcy's life. He half-wished he had not stopped Colonel Fitzwilliam from going after Wickham with a pistol at Ramsgate. What spiteful fate had set Wickham to cross paths with his Elizabeth?

Mention of Wickham always sent clouds of fury through Darcy's mind, making it difficult to think clearly, but not to the degree that he had failed to notice Elizabeth's anger at him. Painstakingly he tried to reconstruct the conversation in his head, hoping to understand why her attitude had changed so much. What had she said about her sister, that she was heart-broken? He dismissed that idea. Miss Bennet had been disappointed by the loss of a fine marital prospect like Bingley, no doubt, but her heart had not been touched. She had never shown signs of a particular regard for him.

But while Elizabeth might profess an opinion not her own, she was not the sort to lie. She must believe that her sister cared for Bingley, perhaps out of her own romantic notions. His anger softened a little at the thought, soon procuring forgiveness for her. But no wonder she was distressed, if she felt torn between her growing affection toward him and her loyalty to her sister.

He nodded slowly. That would explain a great deal.

Elizabeth put down her embroidery with a sigh and rose to her feet. What ill-luck was it that caused Mr. Darcy to come to call on her whenever she was alone? In any case, should he not be at Rosings for tea, along with the Mr. and Mrs. Collins? Elizabeth had pleaded a headache and stayed home, primarily to avoid the gentleman now standing before her.

He did not sit down, but instead paced back and forth across the floor. "I am sorry to hear you have been in ill-health," he said. "May I hope that your headache is better now?"

"Tolerably so, thank you." Perhaps she should have said it was much worse, and then he might go away.

But he seemed to have something else on his mind. He did not appear to be in good spirits; in fact, if anything she would have said he looked worried.

"Miss Bennet. I wish to apologize for my behaviour yesterday." He spoke hurriedly, as if he wished to get the words out as quickly as possible.

The great Mr. Darcy lowering himself to apologize? Hardly likely. Elizabeth wondered what he was hoping to accomplish. Certainly he could no longer be maintaining any romantic intentions toward her.

"There is no need for apologies. It was a misunderstanding, nothing more." She hoped he would go now.

He did not seem happy with her response. "I would also like to ask you to keep what I said about my sister in strictest confidence. I am sure you understand the importance of this."

So he did want something from her. As if she would be likely to reveal something to the discredit of a young girl she did not even know! "You may count on me to reveal nothing, because that is precisely what you told me."

"But about Mr. Wickham...."

"Mr. Darcy, I understand that you and Mr. Wickham have your disagreements, and that one of them apparently involved your sister, but I would prefer to remain outside them."

"*Disagreements*? Is that what he called them?"

Elizabeth was quite exasperated by Darcy's refusal to change the subject. "Difficult as it may be to believe, I do not recall every single word he ever spoke to me, either about his sister or about you, nor do I see any reason why I should tell you if I did."

He fell silent, but the whiteness of his face spoke of his anger. His boots seemed to strike the worn rug with unnecessary force. She could see his struggle to keep control, but sympathized with him not at all. If he insisted on forcing the topic of Mr. Wickham on her, she was well within her rights to say what she did. It was just more proof of his pride and ill-temper.

Finally he burst out, "I cannot believe that you place your trust in such a man."

"I have seen no reason not to."

"He is a scoundrel. He has wasted his education, squandered his inheritance, left debts behind him, and attempted to take advantage of innocent young women. Is that enough reason for you?"

"Squandered his inheritance? He says you denied him his inheritance." Anger had taken over from wisdom in choosing her words.

"That is nonsense. His inheritance was a living which he chose not to accept, and I paid him three thousand pounds in lieu of the preferment. Which he squandered, then had the audacity to apply to me for the living when it became vacant. You cannot blame me, I hope, for refusing."

Elizabeth was taken aback. Their stories coincided, except for the portion regarding the payment. But which man to believe? Mr. Darcy had never seemed a dishonest man, despite his ill-temper, and what would it profit him to make up such a tale? But if he was telling the truth about that, should he also be believed about Mr. Wickham's other supposed sins? She could not imagine that amiable gentleman behaving in the manner Mr. Darcy described, although it was true that he seemed rather free with his money, and had been all too ready to denounce Mr. Darcy on their first acquaintance.

"I cannot believe him so bad," she said, more to herself than to Mr. Darcy.

Darcy's mouth twisted. "I had hoped you would trust my word, but since you cannot, I urge you to appeal to Colonel Fitzwilliam for information, since he has the misfortune to know Wickham quite well, and can confirm all the particulars. Good day, Miss Bennet." He slapped his hat on his head and strode toward the door, turning only once for a last, long look.


Elizabeth was still shaken when Charlotte returned. When asked what was the matter, she said, "I believe you were right about Mr. Darcy's interest in me."

Charlotte beamed. "What wonderful news! A brilliant match, indeed."

Elizabeth shook her head. "No, I fear not. I have thoroughly discouraged him. We have quarrelled twice now. He will not be back."

"*Discouraged* him? Eliza, are you out of your mind? Think of the advantages of such a marriage!"

Elizabeth took Charlotte's basket from her and set it on the table. "Dearest Charlotte, you know I have always wished to marry for affection. All the advantages in the world mean nothing to me next to his abominable pride and manners. I could never love such a man."

Charlotte sank down in a chair and closed her eyes. "Sometimes I forget how young you are, Eliza. How can you look at Jane and still believe love is a good thing? Certainly, it can be wonderful for a brief moment, but more often it causes nothing but pain." The bitterness in her voice could not be missed.

"Just because Mr. Bingley did not prove to be the gentleman we believed him to be...."

Charlotte shook his head. "Wait until you fall in love. You will learn there is nothing that can hurt you more. I would never wish to be in love again."

Charlotte in love? "Again? Have you been keeping secrets from me?"

"I should not have mentioned it. You were still a child when it happened."

"But what happened?"

"There is nothing to tell. I fell in love with a gentleman, a young acquaintance of my father who was always kind to me, but I discovered he cared for someone else. That is the whole of my experience with love, but it was enough to show me the dangers. You cannot imagine the pain of being rejected by someone you love. Have you ever seen Jane in such low spirits?"

"No, I have not." Elizabeth suddenly recollected the look on Mr. Darcy's face, just before he left her. Did he feel the kind of distress Charlotte had, or Jane? Quarrelling with him had seemed such an excellent solution, but she had never considered how he might feel. She had accused him of ignoring her sister's sensibilities, yet she herself ignored his. If Mr. Bingley had treated Jane so, her sister would have been devastated. Oh, why had she not been more gentle in her attempts to dissuade Mr. Darcy from pursuing his suit? She was no better than he in that regard.

Charlotte stood and rubbed her hands together. "But it is all no matter. Love comes to nothing in the end, and life goes on." She left the room quickly, before Elizabeth could respond.

But Charlotte's words continued to echo through Elizabeth's mind. After walking herself into exhaustion on the muddy footpaths of Rosings Park, she perched on the wobbly footstool outside the parsonage's kitchen door to shake off the worst of the dirt from her petticoats and half-boots. She began to scrape the soles of her boots along the bristle-brush left there for that purpose.

A woman's low laughter came from kitchen. Elizabeth recognized the voice of Mary, the maidservant. In her broad Kentish accent she said, "He may be a fine gentleman indeed, but I would not choose to serve such a stern master, no, indeed, I should not!"

"That is all for show," a man's voice replied. "In private he is quite different. If I must be in service, I can think of no better master than Mr. Darcy. He treats us with kindness and generosity, and never makes unreasonable demands. My last master, now, if the mood took him, he would rage at me and blame me for everything, but not Mr. Darcy. If aught troubles him, he just keeps to himself. Almost never does he have a cross word for anyone."

Elizabeth could hardly believe her ears. Of all her beliefs about Mr. Darcy, the most certain was that he was an ill-tempered man. She strained her ears to hear more.

"He was in a temper when he left here yesternoon, and that is a fact," Mary said. "Practically grabbed his gloves from my hand and didn't even wait for me to open the door, he was that glad to be gone."

"Aye, he has been in an odd mood of late." The man lowered his voice a little, and Elizabeth could not hear his next words for several minutes, until he spoke up again. "And he burns 'em. Stays up half the night writing letters, pages and pages, and then he burns 'em. I've never seen the like."

"Letters? Who are they to?" Mary sounded fascinated by the prospect of gossip.

"I've no clue. Like I said, he doesn't trouble me when he's in a mood. I just see the ashes in the fireplace in the morning, and I can tell he tosses and turns all the night away. But I didn't come here to talk about Mr. Darcy."

Elizabeth heard Mary's low laugh, then nothing but silence. Cheeks burning, she tiptoed away. Once she was safely out of earshot, she sank down onto a stone bench. Was Mr. Darcy's suffering because of her? The idea of him, sitting late into the night and thinking of her, made her feel oddly warm.

She wondered what the burnt letters had held, and whether they had been addressed to her. She had never received a love letter, but she could not imagine what Mr. Darcy might say in one. Did he save all the words he kept back in conversation for his nightly letters? Was it words of love that he burned each night? A shiver went through her at the thought.

When Jane's next letter arrived, Elizabeth retreated to her room to read it. Although Jane made an effort to be cheerful, it was clear that her spirits were still not recovered. Elizabeth felt a familiar flash of anger with Mr. Bingley for leading Jane on, but could not stop her thoughts from moving to the man she suspected of being the architect of the plan, Mr. Darcy. Perhaps if he was suffering now at her hands, it was only his just due for what he had done to Jane. But even as she thought it, she knew the falsehood of it. Mr. Darcy's pain would not ease Jane's, and whatever his motives, she doubted that he would have deliberately hurt Jane. He seemed so very protective of his own sister.

That was another mystery. Although she told herself she should respect Miss Darcy's privacy and not think on it, she could not help but wonder from time to time what Mr. Darcy's great secret about his sister was, and how Mr. Wickham played into it. Clearly he felt Wickham had injured his sister somehow…. But no, the discussion had started with the idea of a sister being disappointed in love. Although she had accepted that Wickham was not the man she believed him to be, she could not picture him doing anything too bad. Then again, he had been quick to blacken Mr. Darcy's name. Yet Mr. Darcy's concern seemed to be for *her,* that somehow she would be misled by Mr. Wickham. A sudden suspicion crossed her mind. Mr. Wickham and Miss Darcy? But no, it could not be. Wickham had not spoken of Miss Darcy with any particular affection.

She needed some fresh air to clear her mind. Putting Jane's letter aside, she took her sunbonnet and quietly made her way out the door. She was not yet ready to face Charlotte again.

Usually she walked toward Rosings Park, but today that held too many memories, so she set off down the lane toward the village, stepping carefully to avoid stones and ruts in the road. Hunsford was much smaller than Meryton, only a handful of small houses clustered together. As she reached the first cottage, she heard a small child calling desperately, "No! No! Come back!" A quick glance was all it took to assess the situation, as a boy of perhaps six scrambled into the road in pursuit of a dozen chickens. Clearly they had escaped the coop and were now making the most of their freedom. The boy's chasing was only driving them further away.

With a smile at their antics, Elizabeth hurried nearer, shaking her skirts at the chickens to drive them back. She clucked at them, running back and forth as she herded them toward a gate in the fence. The boy, following her lead, pulled the latch to shut the gate behind them, blurting out his thanks, but Elizabeth felt she should be the one to thank him. The adventure had lifted her spirits.

A deep voice spoke behind her. "You seem to have missed one."

She whirled to see Mr. Darcy, impeccably attired as always, holding a struggling white chicken at arm's length. She could not help but laugh at the incongruity of the picture.

With an attempt at solemnity, she said, "As a rule, chickens prefer not to be held."

Mr. Darcy bent over the stone fence and deposited his

charge in the yard. "So I have discovered, but unfortunately, she seemed disinclined to listen to me when I told her to go back."

The image of the proper Mr. Darcy, giving orders to a recalcitrant chicken as if it were a dog, provoked a peal of laughter from her. She clapped her hand over her mouth, recalling her resolve to be kinder with him. "It was good of you to assist."

"It was my pleasure." He seemed occupied with picking stray bits of down off his black coat. When it was cleaned to his satisfaction, he looked up at her, his expression unreadable.

It was hard to be anything but amused when he stood there so seriously while a white tail feather dangling from the collar of his coat, despite his meticulous efforts. She stepped closer and took his lapel between her fingers, removing the offending item and offering it to him. "It appears you missed one as well."

His lips curved slowly into a smile. She had never stood so near to him when he smiled. It was peculiarly consuming, as if his smile somehow possessed the power to draw her in. She had never noticed the light that could dance in his eyes, either.

His fingers closed over hers for a fraction of a second as he took the feather, but it felt longer as warmth penetrated her thin gloves. Suddenly Elizabeth could think of nothing but how astonishing it was that such a man should feel affection for her, of all people.

Instead of letting the feather drift off in the wind, he tucked it into his pocket. "I thank you."

She bobbed a slight curtsey, not knowing what to make of the strange feelings coursing through her. Quickly she reverted to humour to regain control of the situation. "So, Mr. Darcy, now that we have resolved the pressing problem of the chickens, what shall we quarrel about today? I am feeling generous, so I will allow you to choose the subject."

He raised an eyebrow. "Why should we quarrel?"

She stepped back, feeling somehow more secure with a little distance between them. "Why, it seems to be our daily habit. We have exhausted the subject of our various sisters, so I thought we should have a new bone of contention. Perhaps my cousin, Mr. Collins? No, perhaps not, it might be difficult to find two different opinions on him."

Mr. Darcy threw back his head and laughed. "I should be very surprised if our opinions of him differed. I am still amazed that he managed to convince a sensible woman like Mrs. Collins to become his wife. Can you imagine him proposing on bended knee?"

Elizabeth pressed her fingers hard against her lips until she could trust her voice not to express her mirth. "I am sure I could not say."

His smile disappeared. "Pardon me. I did not mean to trespass on any confidence."

"No, it is not that." But she could perceive he was a little offended, and wanted to see his smile again. "I should not say, but will you promise never to tell a soul?"

"You may rely on my discretion."

She leaned toward him and said in a whisper, "I cannot tell you how he proposed to his wife, but he proposed to *me* only three days earlier. On bended knee."

"To *you?* That man proposed to *you?*" He sounded horrified.

"Yes, and was extraordinarily reluctant to accept no for an answer! Fortunately, he found consolation quickly." She could not believe she was sharing this story with Mr. Darcy, of all people.

He seemed to recover enough to see the humor in the situation. "Extraordinarily quickly, I should say."

Elizabeth wished she had known this side of Mr. Darcy

months ago. Perhaps if she had, she might have welcomed his interest in her, instead of putting him off. She could see that it had been there all along, in some of his teasing at Netherfield, but she had been so blinded by his remark at the assembly that she never saw it.

She would have been flattered had Mr. Darcy shown interest in her at their first meeting. Were it not for his pride, there would have been nothing for her to dislike, and she would never have spoken so warmly of her dislike of him to Mr. Wickham. Instead, how quick she had been to believe Mr. Wickham's stories about him, assuming him to be ill-tempered and missing all of his attractive aspects! She rarely had the opportunity to encounter a gentleman with Mr. Darcy's education and knowledge of the world. She glanced up at him, only to discover him regarding her warmly. It was difficult to pull her eyes away, and her pulses began to flutter.

They had almost reached the parsonage when Mr. Darcy stopped and turned to her, a serious look on his face. "There is something I must ask you while we are still in private."

Elizabeth bit her lip. There was only one question which gentlemen sought to ask ladies in private, but she had not expected this after their quarrels. She did not even know what she would answer. She was still too confused about his character, and it was only in the last few days she had been willing to admit he had any redeeming features at all. How could she consider a proposal of marriage?

He appeared not to notice the heat in her cheeks. "It concerns your sister. I observed her closely at the Netherfield ball, but I saw no signs of particular regard for Mr. Bingley. She appeared to enjoy his company, but no more nor less than that of any other gentleman in attendance. I was certain her heart was not touched."

If Elizabeth had been embarrassed before, it was nothing

compared to what she felt now, after misapprising his intentions yet again, especially when she realized she was oddly disappointed to have been wrong. She took a deep breath, attempting to restore her composure, and reminded herself that Mr. Darcy, however much he might admire her, was unlikely to ever act upon such feelings, especially given his objections to a match between Mr. Bingley and Jane. Her sister's last letter had been full of sadness which Jane had struggled unsuccessfully to hide. And Mr. Darcy had as much as admitted to his part in her unhappiness. How had Elizabeth allowed herself to ever conceive that such a man might be attractive to her, or to forget his abominable pride?

She spoke carefully. "Jane's feelings, though deep, are little expressed. She is very private in matters of the heart."

"Is it your belief, then, that she cared for my friend?"

Elizabeth suddenly wished for nothing more than to be out of his company. She folded her hands behind her back and began to walk again. She heard him fall into step beside her, but she kept her eyes on the path. "I will not violate my sister's confidence, but I assure you I am aware of her heart, and she is not mercenary."

He paused. "I did not mean to suggest she was. Your sister herself is beyond criticism. But a dutiful daughter of ambitious parents might accept a man whom she had no particular affection. Your mother's wishes in the matter were quite clear to anyone who met her. The behaviour of your mother and younger sisters, combined with your family's low connections, made such an association unfavourable for a man of Mr. Bingley's standing. If she truly cared for him, such obstacles might be overlooked, though even then it would be difficult. But I saw no evidence that was the case, and I told my friend as much."

She could hardly believe what she was hearing. How dare he say such things to her, and not even have the grace to look ashamed of himself? His calm countenance suggested he expected her to agree with his assessment of her family, her low connections. Such pride was beyond any she had ever attributed to him in the past. Ill-mannered man! To think she had begun to warm to him!

"I wonder at your troubling to take the time to speak to me at all, Mr. Darcy," she said tartly, "given the many failings of my family and your obvious doubt of my own honesty and knowledge of my sister. Surely you can find someone more *appropriate* to pass the time with. If you will excuse me, sir." She swept past him as quickly as she could, but was halted by his hand on her arm. Enraged, she turned to face him.

"I meant no insult to you, but merely was sharing my honest reservations. Perhaps you might have preferred flattery to the truth, but disguise of every sort is my abhorrence."

"There is a difference, sir, between flattery and gentleman-like behavior. If you wish a polite response from me, look first to your own manners, sir, not those of my family. Mr. Wickham was correct about your abominable pride." She knew those words would hurt him, but in her anger no longer cared. "I hope no one ever injures *your* sister as you have injured mine. Good day, sir." She shook his hand off and hurried through the parsonage gate, away from his disturbing presence.

Darcy did not move as the door to the parsonage slammed shut behind Elizabeth. It was as if all the air had been stolen from his lungs and he would never breathe again. He knew not what infuriated him the most, her criticism of his manners – the nerve of suggesting he did not behave like a gentleman! – her agreement with Mr. Wickham, or her departure without allowing him to respond. Wickham! How could she still believe that cad after what he had told her?

But she had saved the worst for last, without even knowing how hard her arrow would hit its target. That he had hurt her sister, albeit unintentionally, he could not deny. She could not have known that Georgiana had also been deceived by a man she believed she loved, who left her without a backwards glance except for his regret over losing her dowry, or that Darcy was still worried about her loss of spirits. His lively younger sister had turned into a shadow of her old self, and it was all Wickham's fault.

And Elizabeth saw him as doing the same to her sister.

It did not matter that he had believed he was acting for the best, that his actions, unlike Wickham's, had no malicious or selfish intent. Or not much selfish intent, he immediately amended his thought, since his hopes for a match between Bingley and Georgiana could not have helped but to make him more opposed to Bingley's interest in Miss Bennet. To Elizabeth, he was the man who hurt her sister, regardless of the reason, and she could no more forgive him than he could forgive Wickham for what he had done to Georgiana.

He fingered the feather in his pocket, remembering the moment when Elizabeth had touched him to remove it, her face alit as much from her inner spirit as from the sun. He had never stood so close to her before, and he had wanted nothing so much as to taste her lips. He had thought she might have felt the same, but he had been fooling himself.

He turned his feet away from the parsonage and began to walk slowly back to Rosings. There was only one thing for him to do.

The following day, Mr. Collins reported that they were summoned to dine at Rosings again that evening. Elizabeth found herself taking unusual care with her preparations, then laughed at herself for her efforts. What, after all, did she hope to accomplish? Mr. Darcy might notice, but he was unlikely to ever act upon it. And she could not make it through an entire conversation with the gentleman without becoming angry at him.

But when they arrived, the sitting room was empty except for Lady Catherine and her daughter. Elizabeth waited for some mention of the missing parties, and was grateful when Charlotte asked after the two gentlemen.

"They have returned to London," pronounced Lady Catherine. "I assure you, I feel it exceedingly. I believe nobody feels the loss of friends so much as I do. But I am particularly attached to these young men; and know them to be so much attached to me! They were excessively sorry to go! But so they always are."

Elizabeth folded her hands in her lap and lowered her eyes. So Mr. Darcy had left, without even mentioning it to her. Had he thought it of no importance to her? Or was leaving her of no importance to *him*? Perhaps he was just as glad to leave after their quarrels. Any admiration he had for her certainly would not have survived the knowledge of her prejudices and her anger. If only she had guarded her tongue better!

Mr. Collins said, "I am sure they are already missing the delightful company of their dear cousin, Miss deBourgh."

Elizabeth was sure they were missing nothing of the sort, so Lady Catherine's next words came as a shock. "It is true, and although it is not yet official, I would not be surprised to see an announcement in the newspapers soon."

Mr. Collins hastened to make obsequious congratulations to Miss DeBourgh, who looked as if she did not feel the matter deserved celebration. Elizabeth, folding her hands so tightly that her knuckles ached, was glad to have everyone's attention focused on the other young lady, for she was sure no one could miss the heat rising in her cheeks.

It was too late to think about what she might have wished for. She would have to make the best of it, and there was no point in dwelling on such an unpleasant subject. She would think no more of him. With new determination, she looked up and rejoined the conversation.

Elizabeth had never realized how much energy one could expend to avoid thinking about one particular thing, especially when that thing seemed to want to be at the forefront of her mind. After a night of restless sleep and a morning where everything seemed to remind her of Mr. Darcy, she was heartily sick of it. Soon, she told herself, she would be unable to breathe the air, because it would be a reminder of Mr. Darcy, since he also breathed that same air!

Finally she decided that if she could not avoid thinking of him, she would attempt the opposite, and deliberately think of him until she was bored with the entire subject. What, after all, was Mr. Darcy to her? He had admired her, and while she could not help but feel the compliment to herself, there was no reason for that to change *her* opinion of *him*. He was not as ill-tempered or unfair a man as she had thought, but it did not therefore follow that he was a paragon of virtue. He was proud, uncaring of the effect of his behaviour on others, and altogether too concerned with himself. Her feelings were hurt not because she had lost an admirer whose good opinion she desired, but because her injured vanity had wanted more appeasement from him. What better cure for having been named as tolerable, but not tempting, than to receive a proposal of marriage from that same gentleman? But she was not a child who needed someone to tend to her ills. Clearly Mr. Darcy had indeed decided that she was tempting, but that was all. If he had truly loved her, he would not have left her side and the same day become engaged to his cousin. No, his affection, if she could term it such, was a shallow thing, if it could be so quickly forgotten! He, like Mr. Collins, had not regretted her for longer than it took to propose marriage to another woman. She would not regret such a fickle admirer, either.

Having settled the matter to her own satisfaction, and having determined that renewing her dislike of Mr. Darcy was much more satisfying than dwelling on her loss, Elizabeth embarked upon a journey of annoyance with the gentleman. By the end of the third day, Charlotte declared herself heartily sorry she had ever heard of Mr. Darcy or his many faults. Elizabeth, chagrined, began to keep her thoughts to herself once more, which proved to be fortunate, since the following day the gentleman himself, accompanied by Colonel Fitzwilliam, once more called at the Parsonage.

Once her initial shock had worn off, she noticed that Mr. Darcy had returned to his old silent habits. Perhaps he had not wished to make this call, but felt somehow obligated. With a hint of tartness, she said, "We had understood from Lady Catherine that you did not intend to return to Rosings this season."

Colonel Fitzwilliam said, "I do not know why, for we told her we would be but a few days." He winked at Elizabeth. "Sometimes one needs a change of scenery even from a place as charming as Rosings Park."

Mr. Darcy seemed to bestir himself long enough to ask, "Miss Bennet, have you heard from your sister of late? Is she still in London?"

"She is, although she has not written recently." Elizabeth wondered at his interest, after their last conversation. It was no doubt an attempt at civility, but it could be nothing more. Whether he admired her or not, he was engaged to Miss DeBourgh, and that was an end to it.

Elizabeth pointedly turned her attention back to Colonel Fitzwilliam, conversing gaily with him for the remainder of their call, but through it all, she remained uncannily aware of the dark eyes fixed on her from across the room.

She was determined to remain annoyed with Mr. Darcy, so the following day, she was pleased to receive a letter from Jane, which would no doubt provide more ammunition for her pointed dislike of Mr. Darcy, the source of her sister's pain. As soon as she had the opportunity, she collected her bonnet and gloves and went for a long walk where she could take her time in perusing her sister's missive.

What a blow, then, it was to her preconception of the contents, to discover that Jane not only sounded like her old self, with none of the sadness of her recent letters, but almost ebullient. The surprising cause for the change became readily apparent, and Elizabeth read her sister's news with increasing delight, any thoughts of Mr. Darcy quite forgotten in her celebration. She finished the letter and put it away, but it would not do; in half a minute the letter was unfolded again to allow her to bask once again in her sister's happiness. It was at that moment that she heard a familiar voice call her name, and she looked up to see the subject of her earlier ill-humour.

Even Mr. Darcy could not dampen her spirits at that point, so she folded the letter and put it once more away before greeting him with all civility.

He took his place walking beside her and said, "You seem happy today, Miss Bennet."

"I am indeed. I received a letter from my sister Jane, who is in excellent spirits."

"I am glad to hear it."

"Apparently Mr. Bingley came to call at my uncle's house, and she was able to report that he was in good health." Elizabeth stole a sly look at him, to see how he bore it, but he seemed unperturbed.

"Yes, he had mentioned he might do so when I saw him last."

Elizabeth turned to stare at him in surprise. He looked uncomfortable, and shrugged his shoulders at her questioning look. "Did you see him in London, then?" she asked.

"Yes, I did." He seemed disinclined to say anything more.

Her cheeks flushed, Elizabeth fixed her eyes on the path ahead of them. Had Mr. Darcy told Mr. Bingley of Jane's presence in London? It seemed the most likely explanation. But what had he meant by it?

She remembered that she had confirmed Jane's affection for Bingley just before Mr. Darcy's surprising departure for London. And then, on his return, the first question he had asked her was whether she had heard from Jane.

He must have done it. She felt warmth all over at the idea, certain he must see how embarrassed she was. She wished she could thank him, but how could she when he had not admitted to the action? Not to mention that he was engaged to another woman.

It was dangerous to let herself feel warmth toward him. Tightening her bonnet strings, she said, "I understand there is reason to congratulate you, as well."

He gave her a puzzled look. "I do not understand."

He had said he abhorred disguise, but that was another falsehood. "Lady Catherine told us of your forthcoming engagement to Miss DeBourgh."

"That nonsense again?" he exclaimed irritably. "I have no intention of marrying my cousin, now or ever."

"But she said…." Elizabeth reviewed the conversation at Rosings in her mind, and realized that Lady Catherine had neatly avoided stating directly that the two were engaged. A feeling of relief suffused her.

Mr. Darcy's annoyance had not yet faded. "How could *you*, of all people, believe such a thing?"

"I am not in the habit of disbelieving what I am told," she said in confusion, perceiving that he was affronted. In an effort to reduce the tension, she changed back to the previous subject, rashly saying what she had only minutes ago decided not to say.

"I cannot help but thank you for speaking to Mr. Bingley. His visit made Jane very happy."

"Do not thank me. I did nothing more than a friend's duty of confessing my error."

"Still, it was generous of you."

His mouth twisted. "I would not wish Miss Bennet unhappy, nor stand in the way of my friend's joy. The experience of having a sister in pain is not unknown to me."

She stole a glance at him. "I am sorry to hear it."

"When my sister was but fifteen, George Wickham took advantage of her innocence to persuade her that he loved her. His object, of course, was her dowry. It was pure chance that led to their elopement being foiled."

"You need not tell me this, sir," she said uncomfortably.

"I would not wish you to be misled by Wickham's charming manner." There was a bite in Mr. Darcy's voice.

"I do not doubt your word." At least not any longer. The words hung unspoken in the air.

"I am glad to hear it, for I do not wish you to be under a misapprehension. Especially regarding me, when it is clear your opinion of me is not high."

"Mr. Darcy, in truth I find it hard to hold *any* opinion about you for more than a day at a time, since you persist in surprising me, and I hear such differing reports of your character as to confuse me completely."

"Differing reports? From Mr. Wickham?"

She shook her head, then with a sudden urge to tease, said, "I have many sources of information, sir. For example, after hearing Miss Bingley praise the neatness and deliberateness of your letter-writing, I now hear that you are prone to write half the night and then burn the results."

He stiffened, and a flush rose in his cheeks. "There is some writing best consigned to the flames."

"Such as?" She was playing with fire, but for some reason, she had no desire to stop.

"Such as words of ardent admiration directed toward someone who would have no desire to hear them." His voice was oddly flat, and his eyes seemed fixed on the horizon.

She had not expected so direct an answer, and it left her confused, embarrassed, and unable to find words for an answer. But something about the set of his jaw told her of his pain, and she could not bear to be the cause of it. "Unless, perhaps, the lady is in possession of *differing opinions* owing to the many differing reports she hears." She blushed furiously at her forwardness.

He froze and stared at her, his mouth opening as if to say something, but nothing emerged. Elizabeth could not quite hide a self-satisfied smile, but did not meet his gaze. After a moment, he appeared to recollect himself and began to walk again. Elizabeth was beginning to think she had misjudged his words and truly embarrassed herself when he finally said in a somewhat strangled voice, "Indeed."

She could not decide how to interpret that, especially since he seemed to have developed a sudden interest in the line of trees on the horizon. He did not show the pleasure she had hoped he might, leaving her to consider the worst possibilities. Perhaps she had done nothing but convince him she was, like so many others, a fortune-hunter of the worst sort. The thought was intolerable, so with great energy she began to discuss the recent improvements Mr. Collins had made to the parsonage at Lady Catherine's behest. It was the dullest and least flirtatious subject she could devise.

Mr. Darcy made little response, but there was nothing unusual about that.

Elizabeth's words continued to haunt her, bringing flushes of embarrassment to her cheeks whenever she thought of their interchange. She held many a conversation in her imagination with Mr. Darcy where she attempted to turn her forwardness into a light-hearted joke, but found that even thinking of him tended to put her wits into disarray. She was tempted to avoid the grove completely the following morning; but her courage, which always rose with each attempt to intimidate her, would not allow such cowardice.

And so it was that she found her way to the grove before the morning mists had been dissipated by the sun, dew staining the edge of her petticoats. Mr. Darcy was already waiting there, and his countenance warmed at her approach. His appearance relieved her greatest anxiety; had she indeed offended him, all he need do was avoid the grove, but instead he had come to meet her. After a brief murmured greeting, he offered her his arm and they began to walk.

They were but a short distance from the Parsonage when Mr. Darcy said, "Miss Bennet, are you indeed a lady of differing opinions?"

Elizabeth's heart began to race. "I pride myself on never maintaining the same opinion for more than an hour at a stretch," she said with mock solemnity.

He inclined his head. "Then I will have to hope that I am choosing the correct hour to give you this, rather than allowing it to join its fellows as kindling for the fire." He took a letter from his pocket and held it out to her.

Her hand trembling slightly, she took it between her fingers, aware how close to his body it had been lying. She was too embarrassed to meet his eyes, knowing this was an impropriety that could not be ignored.

"I will leave you now," he said quietly, and when Elizabeth automatically held out her hand to him, he took it in a firm grip.

"And now, in the eventuality that I may never have the opportunity to do this again..." He raised her hand to his lips and applied a kiss that was more a caress than a formality. Then he held the back of her hand to his cheek, his dark eyes capturing hers, and Elizabeth forgot to breathe for a long moment.

Darcy released her hand after brushing it once more with his lips. "I wish you good day, Miss Bennet." And then, with a slight bow, he turned again into the plantation, and was soon out of sight.

"Good day, Mr. Darcy," Elizabeth said to his retreating back. As he walked away, she instinctively pressed the letter to her chest., a smile beginning to curve her lips.

She found her way into a private part of the garden where she could not be seen from the parsonage. With the strongest curiosity, she opened the letter, and, to her increasing wonder, perceived an envelope containing two sheets of letter paper, written quite through, in a very close hand. The envelope itself was likewise full. Sitting on a small marble bench, she then began it. It was dated from Rosings, at five o'clock in the morning, and was as follows:

*If this letter is not to be consigned to the flames, I must consider where to begin. I have told you so often in my dreams and in these letters of my ardent admiration of your person, the extraordinary pleasure I derive simply from being in the same room with you, how the sound of your laughter brings warmth into a cold world, how your eyes sparkle when you tease me, that it is easy to forget that I have used nothing more than glances to communicate those sentiments to you in reality. But start somewhere I must, so I will begin at the night of the ball at Netherfield. I was determined to dance with you that night, to have the privilege of your attention for an entire half hour, a prospect as intoxicating as fine wine. For weeks I had remained on the periphery, listening to your conversations, noting at whom you smiled and whose attentions you preferred to receive, what made you laugh, and how you would step in when you felt someone was in danger of being offended. I wanted to understand your magic, what enchantment you used to keep me in thrall, what secret element you possessed that would not allow me to look away; I, who have looked on the greatest beauties of the ton and remained unmoved.*

*I first came to Netherfield shortly after settling my sister's household in London, after the dreadful affair of which you are aware. I have never been much inclined to social events, preferring a quiet night with a few friends to a ball at Almack's, but at that point my disinclination for society was at its greatest. The man who, although we had grown apart, was my oldest friend, had betrayed me in the worst way possible. I was in no mood to make new acquaintances, and anything that smacked of fortune-hunters enraged me. I cared nothing for what anyone thought of me, and felt little pleasure in anything. Then, one day, someone at a party asked my opinion of something. I responded tersely, no doubt rudely, and you turned your fine eyes on me and said, "And at last Mr. Darcy has dazzled the room with his knowledge! We must all be duly grateful." Your laughing voice seemed to make the candles burn brighter, and I became your captive. But every time I attempted to approach you, you seemed to fly away. You refused to dance with me at Lucas Lodge and later at Netherfield during your sister's illness. Thereafter my only delight was to look on you, to hear you speak, to think of you, to dream of you each night.*

*My dearest Elizabeth – and I must hope you will forgive my forwardness in addressing you thus; but since I have written you so many letters that were never to be read, and it is of little matter to the fire how forward the words it burns might be, I have taken that liberty too often to surrender it now, because the sound of your name, the appearance of it coming from my pen, is an addictive delight – you cannot imagine the torment I felt at leaving Hertfordshire, knowing I was unlikely ever to see you again. I doubt I could have found the resolve to do so for my own sake; it was only out of a sense of duty to Bingley that I could force myself to leave the web of bewitchment you had cast upon me. I wish I could say that I forgot you quickly, but it would be a lie; you were my first thought in the morning and my last at night, and you danced through my dreams like a siren I could not hope to escape, nor did I wish to. For a time I thought it would drive me to madness, and I had only just regained some sense of myself when I left London for Rosings, only to find the siren herself at the end of my journey. Even a brief time in your company was enough to place me once again in the gravest of danger, perhaps even more than I had been in Hertfordshire, because now I had the certainty that I could not escape the memory of you. I tried with all my might to stay away, but a teasing Cupid kept throwing you in my path – at church, where I could not attend to a word of the sermon, as all my prayers were of you; when you dined at Rosings, and I knew that all the family expectations in the world could not compensate for the joy I received whenever a smile would touch your lips. I was lost before I began.*

*I would tell you of my longing for you, but those words are not suited for a maiden's eyes; that letter must be fed to the hungry fire, which does not burn as fiercely as my love for you. I could write to you of the depth of my hopeless admiration of you and how it overcame all my scruples, but words of that sort are likely to be as unforgivable as they are unforgettable. I can only tell you of the lessons I have learned from you, my dearest, loveliest, Elizabeth; lessons of the heart, of the error of my ways and my intolerable selfishness in not considering the sensibilities of those I care for, lessons which have made me a better man. They have also made me into a man who will never forget the sparkle of your fine eyes, the delightful turn of your countenance when you spy a victim for your teasing, the extraordinary light you bring into the darkest room; and I will always feel the lack of your presence when I am away from you, even though years and decades may pass. You are a woman in a million, as much for your honesty and sweetness as for your beauty and wit, and it has been my privilege to be a worshipper at your feet. Those are memories I would not surrender for anything, even if they are the only ones I ever have of you.*

*Now you see what only the flames have seen until now. I will understand completely if you treat me as if this letter had never existed; indeed, I deserve no more, and you need not worry that I will importune you further. Your love is a prize I dare not dream of gaining, one too precious for a mere mortal such as myself, but if you find any small part of yourself that is willing to consider my suit, nay, even to tolerate my occasional presence, I pray you will find some way to take pity on me and show me your forgiveness for these words. I will be in the grove each morning, my thoughts filled with you.*

*I will only add, God bless you.*
*Yours, more than my own,*
*Fitzwilliam Darcy*

Elizabeth's feelings on reading this letter were scarcely to be defined. Her cheeks wore a warm blush provoked by Mr. Darcy's unexpectedly passionate eloquence. His attachment incited gratitude; his ardour, a sense of near-disbelief. How badly she had misread his behaviour even in Meryton, taking such a pronounced dislike to a gentleman who clearly saw himself as in her power! Her inclination before reading it was already in his favour, and it was impossible not to be touched by the depth and enduring nature of his attachment, and being touched by it, to feel some of the same warmth toward the writer. She read the letter over and over again, until she was in a fair way of knowing by heart. Finally, with a dreamy smile, she hid the precious letter in her reticule and returned to the parsonage.

An agitated Charlotte awaited her. "Lizzy, wherever have you been? We have been invited to tea at Rosings, and are expected in less than an hour. Mr. Collins has been frantic over your absence."

Indeed, it had grown later in the day that Elizabeth had realized, but the unexpected invitation threw her into a turmoil of spirits. She had thought she had until the next morning to decide on a response to Mr. Darcy, and now she would be face to face with him in a short time – and in front of his family and the Collinses. How could she meet with him in public with the words of his letter ringing in her mind?

She hurried upstairs to change and to bring her hair into some sort of order. She wished she had more time so that she could look her best, but then she laughed at herself. Given what Mr. Darcy had written in his letter, she doubted it would matter to him if she appeared before him in rags. He had forgiven her so many other faults that a hurried toilette could hardly be expected to affect him!

In a short time, she joined Mr. and Mrs. Collins. The walk to Rosings, which might have given her time to calm herself, instead seemed devoted to flutterings of her pulse. Her distraction was such that Mr. Collins bestirred himself to ask if she were quite well, and to caution her on the dangerous of bringing contagious illness into the presence of Lady Catherine de Bourgh. Elizabeth could not help thinking that Lady Catherine would likely prefer a grave illness to the knowledge that she harboured a competitor for Mr. Darcy's affections!

Elizabeth barely knew where to look when they were ushered into Lady Catherine's presence. She dared not glance at Mr. Darcy for fear that her embarrassment would be all too easy for that gentleman to read. Fortunately, visits with that lady did not require thought about conversation, since Lady Catherine invariably directed the discussion in whatever direction interested her. On this day her mind turned to the subject of punctuality, owing to her displeasure with the arrival of the visitors several minutes after the hour specified.

Mr. Collins naturally could not apologize to her ladyship enough for this grave sin, though he sprinkled his expression of contrition with many compliments to both Lady Catherine and Miss DeBourgh. "We can all learn from your most excellent example, Lady Catherine, especially my dear cousin Elizabeth, as our deplorable tardiness was the result one of her exceedingly long rambles. Your ladyship has condescended to warn her of the dangers of this behaviour in the past. Today she left at mid-morning and did not return until an hour ago!"

"Miss Bennet, is this true?" Lady Catherine demanded.

"I am sorry to say it is true, Lady Catherine. I was preoccupied with my thoughts and lost track of the time, and it was most inconsiderate of me. I hope you will find it in your heart to exonerate Mr. and Mrs. Collins for this fault, which was solely my own."

Mr. Darcy's deep voice came from behind her. "The fault is mine. I encountered Miss Bennet on her walk and engaged her in conversation for some time, which caused the delay in her return."

Startled, Elizabeth looked over at him, and her eyes met

his dark, penetrating gaze. His expression was sober, but she thought she could perceive some signs of concern in the manner in which he held his hands, as if he was uncertain what to do with them. Feeling the more than uncommon awkwardness and anxiety of his situation, she said with a smile, "Mr. Darcy is most gracious, as our conversation was not of such great length that I could not have returned in good time, but the subject of his discourse gave me a great deal to ponder about."

Lady Catherine frowned. "What could my nephew possibly have found to converse about with you at such length?"

Elizabeth, realizing that private conversation with Mr. Darcy was a worse sin in her ladyship's eyes than mere tardiness, thought quickly and said, "Oh! It was a matter pertaining to his visit to Hertfordshire last autumn. The people there are unused to contact with a gentleman as discerning and knowledgeable as Mr. Darcy, and could not always perceive his generous motives in offering them his advice regarding the… management of their estates. I assure your ladyship that I now have a much better understanding of the value of Mr. Darcy's opinion on matters of husbandry - " at that moment her voice faltered briefly as she realized the interpretation he might put upon her words, "And I intend, on my return to Hertfordshire, to make certain that his most excellent advice is attended to by all concerned."

Lady Catherine appeared mollified by this. "I am glad, Miss Bennet, to see that you can recognize your betters and learn from them. I am sure my nephew is far more knowledgeable in these matters than the persons with whom you are accustomed to consorting."

"I cannot argue with your ladyship," Elizabeth said, giving Mr. Darcy a teasing look. "His eloquence is enough to convince even those of differing opinions." She was rewarded by the sight of his eyes opening slightly wider in surprise.

To Elizabeth's mingled relief and disappointment, there

was no opportunity for direct discourse with Mr. Darcy during the visit, as Lady Catherine decreed that her nephew should remain by the side of Miss DeBourgh. Elizabeth did not know what she would have said to him had the opportunity presented itself, but she could not deny that she wished it would. Her frustration was eased only when the time came to depart, when, while Lady Catherine was giving endless household advice to Charlotte, Mr. Darcy caught her gaze and his lips shaped the word, "Tomorrow."

Elizabeth anticipated another restless night, but that did not prove to be the case. Once she was abed, she read Mr. Darcy's letter one more time, then folded it and put it under her pillow, and almost immediately she drifted off into a deep sleep.

When her eyes opened the next morning, the sun was already well up in the sky. The previous day's events came back to her, and she realized that Mr. Darcy would have been in the grove for some time already. How could she have overslept, on this of all days? He must think she wanted nothing to do with him. The very thought caused her a sharp pain.

She threw back the bedcovers and began to dress herself as quickly as she could, without even a thought as to what dress she chose. She brushed her hair out from her braid and twisted it into a knot. She wrapped a few tendrils around her finger to give them a touch of curl, and decided that would have to be enough. What would she do if she reached the grove and Mr. Darcy had already left?

She knew Charlotte would be in the sitting room. Not wishing to waste any precious minutes in conversation, Elizabeth crept down the back stairs and out through the kitchen. She headed for the grove at an unladylike pace.

When she arrived, she did not immediately see Mr. Darcy, and her heart sank. Would she have to wait until the following morning? Would he even return the next day after she had failed to meet him today? Then she noticed a dark shape leaning against the trunk of the twisted oak. It was him; his eyes closed and a pained expression on his face.

She spoke his name, and his eyes flew open, a becoming expression of heartfelt delight diffusing over his face. Elizabeth smiled – she could not have done anything else, as her lips seemed to have taken on a life of their own.

Darcy closed the distance between them with a few long strides. "Elizabeth?" he whispered. "I was afraid you were not coming, that I had misunderstood yesterday."

Her mouth suddenly dry, Elizabeth shook her head. "No, I was merely…. delayed."

"Thank God," he said, his voice rough. Before she could realize what he was about, he took her into his arms and pressed his lips to hers.

She had not known that a man's lips could be so warm and tender, and a surprising heat suffused through her. Her entire being seemed to be concentrated in her lips and on the fortunate spot on her back where his hands pressed against her. Her head swam in a sudden delight.

When he finally released her, his breathing ragged, she could do nothing but stare into his eyes. Despite the novels she had read, she had never realized a kiss could make the entire world a different place.

Her stunned silence apparently worried him, as he took her hands in his and said with concern, "Elizabeth? Are you well?"

A smile bloomed on her face. "Quite well. Very well indeed."

His expression relaxed, and he looked younger and happier. "Elizabeth, tell me you will relieve me from my misery and agree to be my wife." When she did not answer immediately, he added with a smile, "Or must I kiss you again until you agree?"

Elizabeth touched her finger to her lips. "You say that if I refuse you, you will kiss me again, so I must assume that if I accept, it would then follow that you would *not* kiss me. You are an unusual gentleman indeed, sir! This presents me with quite a dilemma." She tilted her head as if in deep thought. "Well, I am afraid you leave me no choice but to refuse, since I would be very sorry if you did not kiss me again."

A multitude of expressions passed over his face, first disbelief, then understanding, then a look of deepest happiness. "In that case, Miss Bennet, I look forward very much to convincing you to change your mind."

With a smile, she closed her eyes and tipped up her face. She did not wait long before Mr. Darcy began to practice his skills at persuasion.

# Reason's Rule

*This story is a variation on a variation. I originally wrote two separate versions of* Impulse & Initiative/To Conquer Mr. Darcy *with different endings, depending on the outcome of the scene in the Pemberley library. The publishing world doesn't look kindly on publishing two versions of the same book, so I had to make a choice, though it meant leaving behind some of my very favorite scenes. I've taken this opportunity to provide an excerpt from it. You don't have to read* Impulse & Initiative *to enjoy it. In brief, Colonel Fitzwilliam convinced Darcy to woo Elizabeth. He wins her heart, employing a great many kisses along the way, and the newly engaged couple travels to Pemberley along with the Gardiners.*

ONE PARTICULARLY FINE MORNING Darcy invited Elizabeth to join him in a walk through the park, a suggestion which she immediately accepted with a smile. She knew from experience that they would wander as far as possible from the house, and that he would share some of his preferred places with her, and that they would not return until she had been thoroughly kissed.

As usual, it did not take long for a delightful tension to develop between the two as they descended among hanging woods, to the edge of the stream where it was crossed by a simple bridge. It was a spot less adorned than many in the park, and a particular favorite of Darcy's. Elizabeth paused on the bridge to look down the glen, which allowed room only for the stream, and a narrow walk amidst the rough coppice-wood which bordered it. As she admired the view, it was with no particular surprise, but a great deal of pleasure, that she felt her betrothed's arms slide around her waist. She leaned back against him with a happy sigh, enjoying the feel of his strong body against hers, and thought of how amazingly far they had traveled in the months of their acquaintance with each other, and how astonished she would have been only a few months ago had she known that some day she would find some of her greatest pleasure and comfort in his embrace.

Darcy's thoughts, as often seemed to happen these days, were not far from hers. He nuzzled her hair, enjoying its softness and sweet scent, and thought of how impossible this scene would have once seemed. The idea of a lifetime without the woman in his arms was be a bleak one indeed. "Did you know," he said softly, his mouth at her ear, "that this was one of the places I used to picture being with you, during those months when I did not expect to see you again, but could not bring myself to forget you?"

She tilted her head against his shoulder so that she could look at him. "Very foresightful, I must say," she teased.

He nibbled gently on her ear. "Are you laughing at my suffering, my love? It was not my fault that I was so bewitched by you."

"Does that mean that you believe it to be mine?" she asked archly.

"Completely and totally." He allowed his lips to drift behind her ear, and then down the line of her neck until she shivered in response. "If you had not persisted stubbornly in being so lovely, so witty, so lively, and so generally enchanting, I would never have had such a problem." He remembered the heated dreams he had first experienced during her visit to Netherfield when Jane was ill, in which he had done so much more to her attractive body than he dared think of at the moment.

She smiled playfully at him, and, taking his hand, tugged him to continue on their walk. "I should have realized that such a beautiful day would put thoughts in your head," she teased.

"And you would be correct that the thoughts were there, but personally, I would lay the blame on the loveliness of a certain lady, rather than the day."

"I am not in a position to argue with your understanding of the situation, sir," she said with a laugh.

"My understanding of these matters is excellent, Miss Bennet. After all, I *understood* that you should marry me long before you did." He picked a sprig of light yellow flowers from a nearby bush and tucking it into her hair.

She gave him a sparking smile. "Yes, but had you courted me like this at Rosings, I might have agreed sooner."

"Which part of this courting should I have used then, madam? I somehow imagine that you might have had some objection had I, on one of our walks through the park, taken you into my arms and kissed you passionately," said Darcy, demonstrating his meaning as he spoke.

She was once more breathless when he released her. "I might have found it somewhat surprising, to say the least, if the severe and stern Mr. Darcy were to have behaved in such a manner," she said lightly, "though it likely would have convinced me that I was somewhat mistaken about your impression of me."

"And what would you have done?"

She decided that it would be impolitic to say that he would have found himself on the receiving end of a tongue-lashing that would have made her response to his proposal look temperate. "Before or after the shock caused me to feel faint?"

"Oh, before, definitely; afterwards I would have been far too involved in taking advantage of you to give my attention to anything else."

"I cannot believe that the proper Mr. Darcy would have had such thoughts," she teased.

"The proper Mr. Darcy was having thoughts at Rosings that would still shock you, my love," he said. "Were you not aware that you were living a double life then? During the day, you limited yourself to the occasional impertinent remark, but late at night, my dearest, your behaviour was truly scandalous."

"Really?" Elizabeth laughed. "And am I to assume that you took advantage of my shocking conduct?"

"Assiduously, my dearest, loveliest Elizabeth. It appears that you have also forgotten the times on our walks when, instead of walking silently at your side, I was doing this." He turned, trapping her between him and the trunk of a large tree, his hands resting to either side of her, and leaned in to press kisses along the lines of her neck, sending exquisite fiery sensations through her. She shivered as his lips explored the tender skin below her ear, haunted by the urgent desire to feel his body against hers. Finally their mouths met; he kissed her lightly but enticingly, tempting her to deepen the kiss. She slid her arms around his neck and pulled him to her as her kisses turned teasing in return, and she felt his fingers tangle themselves in her hair, doing battle with the formal styling until it slid down across her shoulders in a mass of unruly curls.

He ran his hands through her hair, letting himself explore the pleasures of her mouth. "You were not quite so delightfully responsive then; my imagination did not range that far - if it had, you might have found yourself in dreadful straits indeed, my beautiful Elizabeth," he murmured, leaning into her so that her back rested against the tree.

The feeling of his strong body against hers sent intoxicating waves of desire tumbling through her that his kisses could only begin to address, and she gasped her pleasure as his lips again began to wander down to the hollows of her shoulders.

With one hand firmly ensconced in her hair, he trailed one finger of the other along the neckline of her gown in a manner which left her making small, inarticulate sounds of pleasure. "Oh, God, Elizabeth," he groaned as his lips began to explore further. "You have no idea what you do to me."

"William," she whispered, half unwillingly, "you mustn't." Somehow she found the resolve to put her hands to his shoulders to urge him away even as her body clamored for more. Reluctantly, he withdrew, only to slide his arms around her waist, letting her lean against him, her head against his shoulder.

"My love," he said with a deep sigh. "You are such a temptation." After a few moments, he pulled away, taking in her disheveled appearance. "My wood nymph," he said with a smile.

She raised an eyebrow. "I must confess, I do *not* recall you behaving in that precise manner when we were in Kent," she said with a saucy smile, beginning to search through her hair for displaced hair pins.

"That simply demonstrates how little you knew of what was in my mind then."

"No wonder you were so silent, then; your mind was quite busily engaged elsewhere, it seems."

"Well, it should be clear now why I felt obligated to propose, after behaving in such an ungentlemanlike manner."

Elizabeth greatly enjoyed his playful mood, and was pleased that he could now tease her about her hurtful words at Hunsford. Perhaps that piece of the past could indeed be put behind them. "We had best return to the house, I believe," she said lightly, but with distinct meaning, pausing to put her hair up again.

"As you wish," he said with rueful amusement. They walked on for a short time longer, and as they drew nearer to Pemberley House, he paused to enjoy a last few moments alone with her. With a smile, he removed a small twig from her hair.

"While I am more than happy to have you be my wood nymph, my dearest, I believe that I prefer to reserve that look for when we are alone," he said warmly. Their eyes met in a lingering gaze. "You are my very dearest love, Elizabeth; I do not know how I ever managed to survive without you," he said, caressing her cheek lightly.

"So long as you do not try to survive without me now, I am content," she responded. It seemed as if she were always wishing to be in his arms these days; it was a constant sense of loss when they were in company and had to keep to a proper distance. She had truly never imagined the powerful force that love could be, that she would ever reach a state where he would be in her every thought, and that she would want nothing more than to be with him, when love itself would be a physical sensation that filled her whenever he was near. *It is an excellent thing,* she thought, *that we do not have to wait for months to marry; it is too hard to be separated already.*

She did not know the extent to which her heart was in her eyes, but the impact of what Darcy saw in them was powerful. After all of the trials of the last year, the separations, the misunderstandings, the long waiting, and the gnawing need he had felt for her, these few days since she had declared her love for him had been like manna from heaven. He was in a constant state of elation; the pleasure that a mere glance from her could give him was beyond his imaginings. He would have been more than happy to send everyone else away from Pemberley, yes, even Georgiana, so that it could be just the two of them, together always, so that he could always feel her near him, her gaze upon him.

Finally they tore their eyes away from one another and entered the house, where the butler informed Mr. Darcy that the post had arrived, and with it two letters for Miss Bennet. She and Darcy glanced at each other regretfully, neither truly wishing to part from the other, but acknowledging that the time had come. "Until later, Miss Bennet," he said with a formal bow.

"Until then, Mr. Darcy," she responded before finding her way to the sitting room to enjoy her letters. She had been a good deal disappointed in not finding a letter from Jane on their first arrival at Pemberley; and now she had two. One of the letters was marked that it had been missent elsewhere. Elizabeth was not surprised at it, as Jane had written the direction remarkably ill.

The one missent must be first attended to; it had been written five days ago. The beginning contained an account of all their little parties and engagements, with such news as the country afforded, as well as her sister's raptures over her dearest Mr. Bingley; but the latter half, which was dated a day later, and written in evident agitation, gave more important intelligence.

*Since writing the above, dearest Lizzy, something has occurred of a most unexpected and serious nature. An express came at twelve last night, just as we were all gone to bed, from Colonel Forster, to inform us that our sister Lydia was gone off to Scotland with one of his officers; to own the truth, with Wickham! So imprudent a match on both sides! But I am willing to hope the best, and that his character has been misunderstood. Thoughtless and indiscreet I can easily believe him, but this step marks nothing bad at heart. His choice is disinterested at least, for he must know my father can give her nothing. Our poor mother is sadly grieved. My father bears it better. How thankful am I, that we never let them know what has been said against him; we must forget it ourselves.*

Without allowing herself time for consideration, and scarcely knowing what she felt, Elizabeth instantly seized the other letter, and opened it with the utmost impatience.

*Dearest Lizzy, I hardly know what I would write. Imprudent as a marriage between Mr. Wickham and our poor Lydia would be, we are now anxious to be assured it has taken place. Though Lydia's letter to Mrs. F. gave them to understand that they were going to Gretna Green, something was dropped by Denny expressing his belief that W. never intended to go further than London, or to marry Lydia at all. My father and mother believe the worst, but I cannot think so ill of him. I grieve to find, however, that Colonel F. is not disposed to depend upon their marriage; he shook his head when I expressed my hopes, and said he feared W. was not a man to be trusted. My poor mother is really ill and keeps her room. As to my father, I never in my life saw him so affected. I am truly glad, dearest Lizzy, that you have been spared something of these distressing scenes; I do not know how I would manage it, were it not for the aid and support of my dear Bingley, who has been everything one could possibly ask in this time of trouble.*

*Our father is going to London in hopes of discovering Lydia. What he means to do, I am sure I know not; but his excessive distress will not allow him to pursue any measure in the best and safest way. In such an exigence my uncle's advice and assistance would be every thing in the world. I can only rely on you, Lizzy, to determine what is best done regarding Mr. Darcy; I know this must be a blow to him, but if he has any advice or thoughts on how W. is to be found, I beg of you to send word to my father immediately.*

Elizabeth's distress on reading this was great, and she scarce knew what to say or how to look. Lydia and Wickham! She grieved for her lost sister, she feared for the well-being of her family - the humiliation, the misery, she was bringing on them all. Lydia was ruined, her entire life and future destroyed; she knew enough of Wickham not to doubt that he had never had any intention of marrying her sister. Mary and Kitty would be left in hardly better condition; no man would ever offer for them after this disgrace.

She herself could only be horrified by the prospect of Darcy's response to this news. The mortification would be nigh unbearable, and such proof of the weakness of her family must make him regret their alliance; and how were they to explain what could not be hidden to Georgiana? This would crush her. She was only now beginning to recover from Wickham's predations; how would she survive watching Elizabeth's family ruined by the same man, and he still running free to continue to devastate innocent lives? Yet it was inevitable that she would have to know. They could not hide the whole Bennet family from her forever. Darcy would not be able to protect his sister from this blow, nor could he himself be protected.

She knew almost at once that she could not do it, could not wreak this level of destruction on two people whom she loved. With an excess of care she refolded the letters and quietly retreated to her room after informing a footman that she would like to see Mr. and Mrs. Gardiner immediately upon their return from Lambton. Once alone her tears began to flow both for Lydia and for herself, and it was some time before she could regain sufficient composure as to recall herself to what must be done.

She went to the door, intending to seek out Mr. Darcy, but after a moment realized she could not face him, that if she had to see him, she would lose her resolve. Going to the desk, she took out paper and pen and uncapped the inkwell. She struggled for a minute over the salutation, torn between intimacy and formality, and in the end decided to have none.

*Pray forgive my cowardice, sir, in writing you rather than speaking this directly. The news which I received today from Longbourn was not good. There is no easy way to say that which must be said: it appears that my youngest sister has eloped with none other than Mr. Wickham - they are now somewhere in London, and apparently Mr. Wickham expressed to a friend that he had no intention of marrying Lydia. You know him too well to doubt the rest. It is obvious to me that an event of this magnitude will have many ramifications for my family, and I believe it is only prudent to consider what its effects might be on yours as well. As I cannot see any outcome, even the best, of this matter that would not cause substantial damage to you and more particularly to Georgiana given your connection to me, I think it appropriate to reconsider the arrangements we have made. I recall that you at one point extracted from me a promise that I would not break our engagement, to which I agreed unless you should change your mind, but we had no way to foresee a crisis of this magnitude at that time. Had I not made such a promise, it would be clear what my action should be at this juncture; as it is, I can only offer to make this as simple as possible for you. I shall assume unless I should hear otherwise from you that you agree that wisdom must come ahead of wishes at this time. You may, of course, explain this to Georgiana in whatever way you see fit. I will be speaking with Mr. and Mrs. Gardiner to arrange our removal from Pemberley as soon as possible. For my own sake, I ask that we not meet again before I depart.*

Tears overcame Elizabeth once more, and she had to pause for some time before she found the strength to continue.

*Please be assured that I regret this outcome more than I can possibly say, and that you will be ever in my thoughts and prayers.*
*E. Bennet*

She pushed the missive away with shaking hands and buried her face in her handkerchief. She could not tell how long she sat weeping; at one point, a maid came to tell her that Mr. Darcy was looking for her, and she managed to express a wish that Mr. Darcy be informed that she was suffering from a headache and wished to rest. Finally, she reached a point of numbness where all she could do was await the arrival of her aunt and uncle, and hope that it would be soon enough that they could depart that very day.

When a maid finally announced the Gardiners, Elizabeth took up the letter she had written and placed in it the ring Darcy had given her. Folding the paper carefully around it, she instructed the maid to give it directly to Mr. Darcy. *It is done,* she thought. *It is over.*

Mrs. Gardiner, seeing the evidence of tears on her niece's face, immediately put her arms around her, inquiring as to the cause of her distress. Unable to speak, Elizabeth directed their attention to Jane's letters, which they read with some alarm. Though Lydia had never been a favorite with them, Mr. and Mrs. Gardiner could not but be deeply affected. Not Lydia only, but all were concerned in it; and after the first exclamations of surprise and horror, Mr. Gardiner readily promised every assistance in his power. Elizabeth thanked him with tears of gratitude while she wondered desperately how Darcy was reacting to her letter. She could only hope that it was with understanding and forgiveness rather than condemnation and relief at his narrow escape from disgrace.

As they began to consider how to settle matters relating to their journey, Mrs. Gardiner asked, "What says Mr. Darcy to this?" She was somewhat surprised that he would leave Elizabeth to herself in a time of such distress, but could only assume that there must be some explanation.

"I have informed him of our urgent need to depart," said Elizabeth, her voice showing a slight quaver. "I have no doubt that he understands the necessity."

The Gardiners exchanged puzzled glances. There was clearly more here than they were being told, but they saw nothing to justify further inquiry. Mr. Gardiner began to opine that it would make the most sense to start the journey in the morning when they would all be fresh, when Darcy himself appeared in the doorway, his face pale and his lips tight, clearly in the grip of some powerful emotion. Without so much as acknowledging the presence of the Gardiners, he strode over to Elizabeth, who averted her eyes, unable to tolerate the sight of his pain and anger. He held up his hand, holding her letter, now crumpled into a ball, and said fiercely, "No. I do *not* release you, now or ever." He took her hand and somewhat roughly pushed the ring back on her finger. He took her chin in his hand and forced her to look at him. "And this," he said, kissing her deliberately - more in anger, it seemed, than in passion - "is to ensure that, should you be tempted to break your word, your aunt and uncle will be aware that you are already too compromised to do anything but marry me. Do I make myself clear, madam?"

Elizabeth, too numb at this juncture to know whether she was more relieved or distressed by his uncompromising insistence, could only nod dumbly. Darcy released a long breath, and some of the tension escaped from his body. "Now," he said, a little more mildly, and including the Gardiners in his address, "tell me what you know of this matter. What has been done, what has been attempted, to recover Lydia?"

"Perhaps you would prefer to read for yourself," Mr. Gardiner said coolly, holding out Jane's letters. "And, Mr. Darcy..." he paused for a moment, "I do not believe that Lizzy is in a state to deal with your anger at present."

Darcy halted in his attention to the letters, and turned his gaze toward Elizabeth. "No, perhaps not," he said more gently, taking her by the hand. She closed her eyes, desperately wanting his forgiveness and affection, and barely able to keep from sobbing. Darcy began reading once more, his expression indicating his displeasure with the contents of the second letter in particular. "Well," he said with distaste, "it is clear what must be done. I will travel to London in the morning and take care of the matter."

Distraught, Elizabeth said, "Take care of the matter? How? Nothing can be done; I know very well that nothing can be done. How is such a man to be worked on? How are they even to be discovered? I have not the smallest hope. It is every way horrible!"

"Elizabeth, there is nothing easier in the world than working on Wickham. All it takes is money. If I know Wickham, he will not be hiding so much as waiting to be discovered so that he can make his demands. You know that I have dealt with him before, and I can do so again."

She looked at him with eyes filled with pain. "I cannot ask it of you. You cannot take on the mortification of this; it is a matter for my family."

Mr. Gardiner broke in at this point. "Lizzy, your concern for Mr. Darcy is admirable, but I must point out that we are not in a position to turn away any assistance in this matter. Mr. Darcy, if you have information that may be helpful in locating him, I myself would be most appreciative of your sharing it."

Elizabeth took a deep breath, trying to bring herself to some sort of composure that would permit her to participate reasonably in this discussion. "Uncle, there are connections between Mr. Darcy and Mr. Wickham of which you are unaware, and this has nothing to do with him."

"This has *everything* to do with me, Elizabeth!" Darcy exclaimed irritably. "Why do you suppose this happened? Wickham must have heard of our engagement - this is just what he tried last summer, but now he is trying to strike at me through you. Your sister has nothing to offer him; she is but a pawn in this game, and he is after either money, or revenge, or most likely both. If you break off our engagement, you will be giving him exactly what he wants - the ability to take away from me that which is most dear!"

She stared at him in horror. She had not thought so ill, even of Wickham, as to think that his hatred would extend so far. Darcy, misinterpreting the look on her face, said with bitter regret, "You cannot know how sorry I am to have brought this upon you; I hope that someday you will be able to forgive me."

"You have done nothing to cause this," she said fiercely, astonished that he could think that she blamed him for these events. "You are not responsible for Wickham's behaviour, nor for Lydia's, and I will not have you fault yourself for it!"

Her unexpected defense of him was the first positive indication Darcy had seen that she cared for him still, and he took her into his arms gratefully, heedless of the presence of her aunt and uncle.

Mr. Gardiner cleared his throat. "I am beginning to feel like an actor who is onstage without having read the script. There is clearly more to this story than I know, and I wonder if there is not someplace more appropriate than Lizzy's bedchamber to be having this discussion."

Darcy released Elizabeth with reluctance. "You are correct, sir, it is time that we pool our knowledge. Perhaps we could discuss this further in my study; it is a conversation I would prefer to have behind closed doors, for reasons which will become clear."

Elizabeth was feeling such relief that she found it difficult to focus on the question of Lydia; all she wanted was to return to Darcy's arms and stay there forever. That could not be, though. She knew Mr. and Mrs. Gardiner had no intention of leaving Darcy alone with her in her bedchamber for even a minute. "I will join you shortly," she said.

Darcy, who was not at all ready to let her out of his sight, looked at her with concern. She smiled wanly at him, and said reassuringly, "I require a moment to make myself presentable, sir; that is all."

His countenance cleared somewhat. "I will expect you in five minutes, no more," he said, his tone clearly communicating to her his need to have her by his side.

Mrs. Gardiner shooed her husband along with Darcy. "I will stay with Lizzy; you go ahead and talk about whatever it is that men talk about."

Once they had left, she turned to Elizabeth. "Lizzy, my dear, that looked quite worrisome. You look very ill."

Elizabeth poured water from the ewer into a basin and began to rinse her eyes. "I am well enough, aunt. I am afraid that when Mr. Darcy and I disagree, we tend to do so with a certain ferocity that cannot be pleasant to observe, and both of us have been known to say some quite hurtful things in the heat of the moment. Fortunately, we are also both quite forgiving of the other."

"I do not understand. I take it that you told him that you wanted to end the engagement - that suggests more than a mere disagreement, Lizzy, and he was very angry," Mrs. Gardiner said gently.

Elizabeth sighed. "It was because of Lydia; I did not want to taint him with the disgrace we face."

"Oh, Lizzy. And he is so attached to you - I cannot say that I think that was wisely done, my dear."

"I do not want his reputation to suffer because of me!"

"And you do not trust him sufficiently to speak to him about your fears."

Her aunt's insightful comment cut closer than Elizabeth cared to consider at the moment. She dried her face. "I did promise to be down in five minutes, and I suspect that I had best be prompt. Shall we join the gentlemen, then?"

"If you are ready, we certainly may," answered Mrs. Gardiner. She had noted her niece's discomfort, and hoped that she would think further on what she had said.

Darcy and Mr. Gardiner were already ensconced in the study when the ladies arrived. Darcy opened the discussion by detailing his connection with Wickham, including the events of Ramsgate. Although Elizabeth had already given them to understand that Wickham was not to be trusted, the extent of his dissipation came as a surprise to Mr. and Mrs. Gardiner.

"I have some connections still which may assist me in locating Wickham," Darcy said. "Once I reach London, I will begin to explore the possibilities. Obviously, I will need to consult with Mr. Bennet. Where would I be most likely to find him?"

"I do not doubt that he is staying at our house on Gracechurch Street," said Mr. Gardiner, "and I am inclined to think that I should accompany you, as I am familiar with London in a way that Mr. Bennet is not, and possibly more able to negotiate with Mr. Wickham."

Darcy shook his head decisively. "I shall handle the dealings with Wickham. Your assistance, however, in working with Mr. Bennet might be very helpful; he has felt little reason to trust me in the past, and I doubt these events will have improved the situation."

"Would it be possible, then, for Mrs. Gardiner and me to proceed directly to Longbourn? Jane, I believe, must be in need of our support with my mother," said Elizabeth.

Darcy turned an enigmatic gaze on her. "I would prefer to have you in London, Elizabeth."

"In London? I cannot see what that would accomplish."

"I may need your assistance in handling Lydia. I doubt that she would be inclined to listen to me," he said. "And I would appreciate your presence. Jane is not without resources; Bingley is there with her."

Elizabeth's concern about Jane did not abate, but as she opened her mouth to object once more, she saw the beseeching look in Darcy's eyes. Thinking of her aunt's earlier words about trusting him, she agreed to the plan with uncharacteristic meekness.

Plans were soon set; Darcy offered to send servants with Mrs. Gardiner to Longbourn, while Mr. Gardiner and Elizabeth would travel to London in Darcy's carriage.

As the conversation drew to a close, Darcy felt himself becoming unaccountably nervous, not so much regarding the trip to London, but rather about the inevitable tête-à-tête with Elizabeth. His initial anger with her had dissipated, but he feared what her response would be to his harsh words, and his own sense of injury that she would have even contemplated that he would wish to end their engagement was vivid. Did she still have so little idea of what she meant to him? Did he mean so little to her? He knew that he could not expect reassurance from her given her own level of distress over her sister, yet it would be difficult, if not impossible, for him to disguise his own feelings.

Mrs. Gardiner was not unaware of the tension between the two, and at the earliest opportunity, she extracted her husband from the room, leaving Darcy and Elizabeth alone. Mr. Gardiner departed only after a hard look at Darcy which carried a distinct warning of how he would view any further behaviour that distressed his niece.

Silence fell between the two. Elizabeth fixed her eyes on her folded hands as if seeking to deny any involvement in this unhappy affair. Darcy's dark gaze was on her, the pain he felt evident in his look, but also mingled with sympathy. He could recognize her silence and averted eyes from past times when she had felt ashamed of her behaviour toward him.

"Elizabeth," he attempted, "I should not have said what I did earlier, at least not in the way I did. My disposition is such that when I lose my equanimity I am prone to speaking before I think; I have tried, with some success, to moderate this, or at least to prevent it from happening in the first place. I apologize that I was unable to do so today."

She looked up at him tentatively, relieved that he did not seem inclined to berate her. "I did not intend to anger you," she said, wishing that she could say more, but unsure how even to begin.

"Do you regret my refusal to release you from your promise?" he said abruptly. He had not meant to ask it, and certainly not so harshly, but the words came out despite his intent.

"No," she responded in a heartfelt manner to his great relief. "My action represented my concern for you, not a lack of feeling. Please do not think that it signifies any second thoughts on my part."

"What *am* I to think, given that the moment we run across an obstacle, your first reaction is to sever all contact between us? How should I feel, knowing that you believe that I feel so little for you that I would be prefer never to see you again rather than to tolerate someone I dislike?" His voice reflected the depth of his frustration and pain. "My desire to marry you is not a whim of the moment, Elizabeth."

"I never thought that it was," she said, once again near tears.

Darcy cursed himself for upsetting her again. He knelt next to her chair and took her hand in his. "Elizabeth, my dearest love, please believe me when I tell you that there is nothing more important in the world to me than you, and your love is my most valued treasure. I would not give you up for anything."

Her eyes, luminous with unshed tears, met his, and she put her arms around him. "I will try to trust in that more," she whispered into his shoulder.

He picked her up and settled her on his lap, where she relaxed into the comfort of his arms with the relief of the resolution of their disagreement predominant in her mind. She felt exhausted by the emotions of the last hours - their closeness on their walk, the shock of Jane's letters, her distress over their future, his anger, and her aunt's criticism all combined to leave her feeling as if she had been buffeted in the wind.

He said softly in her ear, "Do you know how much you frighten me when you withdraw from me? I need you beside me, Elizabeth; I need your affection and warmth."

She looked up at him. "It frightens me, too," she said quietly, her face speaking the truth of her statement.

He captured her lips with his in a kiss that spoke more of a need for reassurance than of passion, a need that it met for both of them as they sought to erase their pain and fear in one another's arms. "I do love you, William," she said, stroking his tousled hair, when he released her. "On that you may depend."

"Elizabeth, my dearest, you cannot know what that means to me. Thank you for agreeing to come to London."

"I am not certain *why* I agreed, apart from being able to discern that you wanted me to be there."

"And is that not reason enough?" he teased. "My reasons for wanting you there are mostly selfish, my love. Dealing with Wickham will be painful and unpleasant, and being able to spend time with you will ease that, and also - well, it is not reasonable, I know, but I would worry if you were as far away as Longbourn. It will be hard enough having you in a different part of the city after this week together."

"Why would you worry?"

"I said it was not reasonable, did I not? I would worry about losing you somehow, and I must warn you that I am likely to become irritatingly protective of you now that Wickham has tried to hurt me through you."

She stroked his cheek lightly. "William," she said hesitantly, "why does he dislike you so?"

Darcy sighed and pulled her close to him. "I suppose that is a fair question, given that you are now involved in the matter, although I cannot say that I enjoy speaking of it. It is not simple to explain, either. We were friends as boys, as you know, and I do not think that he ever forgave me for growing up. When we were young, we tended to a certain degree of wildness; we did what we pleased and were always into one mad scrape or another, and we usually could avoid any consequences, he, because he could charm his way out, and I because of my name. But at a certain point I began to realize that I had responsibilities, ones that did not include playing pranks on the unsuspecting, and I began to try to control my impulses more. It was about this time that I was sent off to school, which was the first time he seemed to feel the difference in our stations, and I believe that he was quite angry to recognize that I had prospects that he did not, and that I was leaving him behind. When I returned after my one year at school, I had become much more serious, and my mother's illness only added to that. He would have grand ideas for adventures for us, and I would choose to sit with my mother instead; this angered him as well. He seemed to set himself to excel wherever I did not, and strove to be everyone's favorite. He was charming and amiable where I was the proverbial dull boy; he could make my father believe anything, usually to my detriment, but when all was said and done, I was still heir to Pemberley, and he was merely to have the living at Kympton."

He paused, raking his hand through his hair. "It is not as if he is my nemesis, or even particularly evil, you understand. He is feckless, impulsive, and an opportunist par extraordinaire, and he can improvise on any situation at a moment's notice. I do not believe that he spends his time devising ways to hurt me, but he cannot resist sticking in the knife whenever an opportunity presents itself. You saw him in action in Meryton; it was purely coincidence that our paths crossed there, and it profited him nothing to malign my name, but he could not resist the opportunity. It was only my ill fortune that he happened to pour his venom into the ear of someone whose good opinion I desired; I have no doubt that his satisfaction was merely to have everyone dislike me and admire him. Georgiana was an opportunity for quick money for him more than anything else; had he succeeded, he would have enjoyed watching how much I hated what he had done, and I am sure he would have derived great pleasure from forcing me to treat him as an equal if he married my sister, but his primary motivation was her dowry. He has always loved money and profligacy. I doubt that he made a great plan to inveigle Lydia into eloping with him; I suspect that he merely saw the opportunity and could not resist it."

As he spoke, Elizabeth could hear the pain of betrayal behind all of his carefully reasoned words, and suspected that Wickham was not the only one haunted by the ghosts of that early friendship. She stroked his cheek gently. Impulsively, she said, "Thank you for loving me enough to allow me a second chance."

"How could I not love you? I tried not to love you, but it was not to be; I have been yours for a very long time. Even had you refused to have anything more to do with me, I could never have stopped loving you."

She could think of no answer for this but a lingering kiss, which she broke off abruptly as a thought came to her. "What are we going to tell Georgiana?" she asked with dismay.

Darcy frowned. "I shall tell her that I have to go to London on business, and that you are accompanying me, I suppose."

"She will have to know the truth sooner or later," Elizabeth said hesitantly. "She dislikes being treated as a child; perhaps we should trust her in this."

His first thought was to contradict her, but then he thought better of it, recalling that one of his hopes for Elizabeth was that she would understand Georgiana more readily than he did. Still, it went against the grain not to protect his sister from unpleasantness, particularly when it touched so closely on her. Finally, he asked slowly, "Do you think that would be best?"

"I believe so, but you know her better than I."

"Your instincts with her are better," he replied, thinking how little he wished to raise the subject of Wickham with his sister. "Would it be cowardly to ask you to tell her? She will likely be more open with her feelings to you."

"If you wish," she said. "Perhaps I should talk to her now, so that she has some time to take it in before we leave."

Darcy was less than happy with the idea of allowing Elizabeth to leave. He felt that she had not yet recovered herself from the shocks of the day; he wished that she would smile, or show him that sparkle in her eyes, so that he could feel secure of her state. Perhaps it was too much to ask, though. "I suppose that makes sense," he said, kissing her forehead, "much though I would prefer to keep you here in my arms."

"Sooner or later someone is bound to walk in," she replied practically. "We have been fortunate thus far."

"I bow reluctantly to your wisdom," he said, releasing her. As she headed past the door, he added, "And, Elizabeth..."

"Yes?"

"Do not try to end the engagement again, even should you be convicted of murder and awaiting hanging in Newgate Prison. I do not want to hear ever again that you are worried about damaging my reputation in some way."

She smiled in amusement. "I shall keep that in mind, William, though at present I can assure you that I have no particular plans to murder anyone."

Georgiana took the news as well as could be expected. There were some tears, and a little of the stiff Darcy pride that Elizabeth knew hid feelings too painful to expose to the world. When

Georgiana requested some time to herself to consider the matter, Elizabeth encouraged her in finding her own strength, and honoured her request.

She considered hiding in her room again herself, but brooding would not be helpful at this stage; she needed to save her strength for the days ahead. With a sigh, she collected her embroidery and returned to the study. Darcy was only too happy to have her companionship and, after asking after his sister, returned to the papers he was obligated to complete before their departure on the morrow.

Elizabeth was content to sit quietly as she worked, but eventually thoughts of Lydia began to intrude despite her best efforts to discourage them. She had grave fears for her sister's future - even if Wickham could somehow be brought to marry her, what sort of future could she have, as a wife to such a wastrel? Lydia had never learned to consider the consequences when choosing her pleasures, and now the consequences would be dreadful indeed, not only for herself but for her entire family. How could Lydia have been so heedless as to behave in such a brazen manner?

Yet how could Elizabeth condemn her completely when she herself had permitted liberties so far beyond the proprieties herself, when she herself had behaved in a shameless manner when confronted by temptation? She was equally at fault, only more fortunate in the outcome; she had taken the similar risks to her own reputation and that of her family each time she had allowed Darcy to touch her. A sense of shame began to gnaw its way through her.

She stared blindly at her embroidery. *No better than Lydia,* she thought, the words burning her like acid. She could not even bring herself to look in Darcy's direction. Feeling the need to escape, she stood suddenly, drawing his attention. "Please excuse me," she said. "There is something I must fetch."

Darcy was puzzled. "Elizabeth, wait, please," he said, noticing the lines of stress in her face, and wondering if she could be trying to run away again. "Something is troubling you, I can tell. Will you not tell me about it, my love?"

Elizabeth knew that she was caught, and it gave her a moment of panic. "It is nothing that requires attention," she said anxiously.

He sat back, looking at her unhappily, wishing he knew how to convince her to confide in him. "Can you trust me enough to let me be the judge of that?" he said as gently as he could manage.

*And you do not trust him sufficiently to speak to him about your fears.* Her aunt's words came back to her, and she paused in indecision. He would want her to tell him, she knew, but she was far from wishing to share these thoughts. She certainly did not want to draw his attention to the similarities between herself and Lydia - she could imagine the expression of distaste he would have on his face. Yet if she could not have faith in him not to reject her, perhaps it was best to discover it now. With a sense of fear looming, she said half-unwillingly, "I was seeking privacy, sir, because I have been reviewing my own behaviour in light of these events and finding it wanting."

Her distant form of address worried him. "What behaviour do you have in mind? I can think of none that has been wanting in any way."

"I see little difference in Lydia's heedless behaviour and my own..." she paused, her face pale, "my own shameless conduct of recent weeks. It is not a comfortable conclusion."

He rose and came to her, taking her hands in his. "It is a very *questionable* conclusion, in my opinion. How can you compare the two? Your sister's reckless decision to elope rather than to approach your parents about marriage, and with a man she barely knew - how does that balance against allowing a few liberties to a man who has already declared his intentions, whom you had known for some time, and to whom your family had social connections? I cannot imagine that if I had asked you to elope in the first days of our acquaintance, you would have done anything but laugh at me! Would you have permitted my kisses if you did not know my intentions?" His earnestness was apparent.

"No," she said with a small smile. "You are correct, I would not have done so. But I did risk both my reputation and that of my family, as we saw in Hertfordshire."

"If we are to impose blame for that behaviour, I believe that *I* deserve more than an equal share! All the same, you knew that the risk was not serious, that if there were any compromise, I would marry you, and you knew that my credentials as a potential son-in-law were good. We may have been imprudent, my love, but hardly reckless - hardly the equivalent of what Lydia and Wickham have done. Our situation was unusual, after all - that you had refused me but were still allowing me to court you - and the usual rules for pre-engagement behaviour are difficult to apply in such a circumstance. You could hardly pretend to be unaware of my interest in you!" He looked at her challengingly.

"Perhaps I did assume too far," she allowed. "You are very good to me, William."

"Just because you are soon to become a Darcy does not mean that you need to challenge us in the art of jumping to conclusions, my love," he said teasingly. As his comment finally drew a natural smile from her, he embraced her gently. "Besides, I do not believe that I ever touched you just for my amusement; I did so when the alternative seemed to be leading me down the road to Bedlam."

Elizabeth gave him a sidelong look. "I hardly think you were at that grave a risk," she said.

"Do not think to test that theory now, madam," he replied lightly. "My need for your kisses still borders on the desperate."

She smiled as he leaned down to capture her mouth in an affectionate kiss.

It came as a surprise to all concerned when Georgiana made the determined announcement at dinner that she intended to accompany them to London. Darcy, making a valiant effort at not refusing out of hand, glanced over at Elizabeth, who nodded slightly. Finally he said, "If that is what you wish, then, I see no reason to refuse. I must warn you, though, that this trip will be strictly business - there will be no time for outings or other pleasures."

Georgiana acknowledged the point, but insisted on following her plans. Later, when she was able to speak to Elizabeth privately, she thanked her for her support. "I know that William would have never agreed to it on his own, and I do want to go. It is not that there is anything I can do to help, but I do *not* want to spend the rest of my life trying to avoid whatever part of the country he might be in. This seems as good a time as any to face my fears."

Elizabeth embraced her. "I am glad that you have found that courage. That is the first step to healing."

"I cannot help but think that it could have been me, but for the chance of William's arrival," she said softly. "I was such a fool. *You* would never have been taken in so, Elizabeth."

"I beg to differ, I spent a good deal of time in Mr. Wickham's company, and I was quite taken with his amiability and manners. I even believed lies that he told me about your brother," Elizabeth said ruefully.

"I find that hard to believe!" Georgiana exclaimed, then, realizing what she had said, timidly retreated, saying, "I do not mean to doubt your word, Elizabeth; it is only that it surprises me."

Elizabeth shook her head. "It seems we are all vulnerable to having our hearts lead us astray from what is right," she said, thinking of the principles she had violated in her behaviour with Darcy.

"Some of us more than others," said Georgiana wistfully.

They set out early the next morning in the elegant Darcy travelling carriage, quite possibly the most comfortable conveyance in which Elizabeth had ever ridden, and certainly the fastest. Conversation was somewhat stilted for quite some time, as the subject which preoccupied three of the travellers -- the plans for London and ideas for how to discover Wickham and Lydia -- were unsuitable for the fourth. Georgiana, acutely aware of the fact that her presence was inhibiting the others, became even more reticent than usual.

They travelled as expeditiously as possible; and after sleeping one night on the road, reached Gracechurch Street the following evening. Elizabeth exited the carriage with relief after the long ride. Darcy joined her, as he hoped to speak with Mr. Bennet regarding his plans.

Mr. Bennet looked years older than he had when they had left Longbourn. Elizabeth, concerned by her father's appearance, moved to embrace him. A quick exchange of words established that there had been no progress in the matter of discovering Wickham and Lydia.

"Mr. Bennet, may I have a word with you?" asked Darcy formally. "My sister is waiting in the carriage, and I would like to take her home as soon as possible."

Mr. Bennet, curious, ushered him into the sitting room. "Well, Mr. Darcy, if I am surprised to see my daughter tonight, I am quite baffled as to what brings you here." He would have thought that under the circumstances, Darcy would be keeping the greatest possible distance from the Bennet family, and had in fact had moments of concern over Elizabeth's engagement to him.

Darcy wasted no time. "Mr. Bennet, it is late, and I have much to discuss with you. If it is agreeable to you, I would like to call on you tomorrow morning to discuss the current situation. I have some ideas as to how I may be able to locate your daughter Lydia, but I would like first to become current on all the information you may have regarding her elopement and Wickham's situation. We need to discuss as well the arrangements you will authorize me to make for her once I have settled matters with Wickham."

Mr. Bennet was exhausted from long days and nights of anxiety and self-recrimination, and was coming to a point of despair on the matter. Darcy's brash assumptions irritated him, and his ability to disguise his feelings was rapidly slipping. "So, Mr. Darcy, you propose to walk in, find Wickham and Lydia, make all the arrangements and solve all the problems. Do I have that correctly, or have I missed some points on your agenda?"

*I should have asked Mr. Gardiner to join us,* thought Darcy as his anger rose. *I should have known that we would be at odds in a matter of minutes..* Struggling to keep his ire in check, he said in a cold tone, "You have it correctly. I had thought you would prefer to be consulted; if that is not the case, it will be simpler all around for me to proceed unilaterally on this matter."

"You are very confident of yourself, Mr. Darcy." Mr. Bennet's manner matched Darcy's for coolness.

Darcy knew that his ability to control his anger was reaching its limits. "I am confident that I stand the best chance of discovering Wickham and bringing matters to a satisfactory conclusion. Perhaps your daughter or Mr. Gardiner can apprise you of my plans in a manner that interests you more. I shall be in contact when I have information for you, then. Good evening, Mr. Bennet." He swept out of the room.

Finding Elizabeth without, hoping for an opportunity to bid him farewell, he took her by both hands. "My love, you will have to teach me patience," he said regretfully. "I fear that your father could make a saint curse, and I am no saint."

"Why, what is the matter?" she asked with concern, unable to see any grounds for a disagreement.

"He is not interested in my assistance. It seems that he thinks that I am brash and overconfident."

Elizabeth touched his cheek. "Oh, William. I am so sorry."

Darcy sighed. "It is of no matter. I will proceed on my investigations, and perhaps he will find results more convincing than words. In any event, I hope to be able to call tomorrow, but if I am unable to, I will send word."

"I will be thinking of you," she said softly, conscious of how much she would miss him, after becoming accustomed to spending much of her days with him.

He raised her hands to his lips. "My dearest love, you will be in my thoughts every moment." Their eyes locked, speaking volumes, until Darcy saw a movement out of the corner of his eye.

Mr. Bennet stood in the doorway. "I have spoken with my brother Gardiner, and he suggests that I may have been overhasty in spurning your assistance, Mr. Darcy," he said in a voice which bespoke his dislike of the situation.

Elizabeth looked up at Darcy anxiously, hoping he would accept this overture. He tightened his grip on her hand briefly, then said levelly, "If there is assistance I can offer, it is yours."

"Perhaps, as you suggested, we could meet tomorrow to share what we know."

Darcy bowed. "I shall be here, sir." He turned to Elizabeth, and said, "Until tomorrow, then." He dearly wished to be back at Pemberley, where he could speak to her more freely.

Her gratitude for his patience showed in her eyes. "Good night, William," she said softly.

He took his leave, and Elizabeth turned to her father. "You look very tired. I am sorry for what you must have endured here," she said sympathetically.

He grimaced. "Say nothing of that. Who should suffer but myself? It has been my own doing, and I ought to feel it."

"You must not be too severe upon yourself," replied Elizabeth.

"You may well warn me against such an evil. Human nature is so prone to fall into it! No, Lizzy, let me once in my life feel how much I have been to blame. I am not afraid of being overpowered by the impression. It will pass away soon enough."

"You at least need not be alone in this any longer," she said.

His mouth quirked in a smile. "I confess I am glad to have you here, Lizzy, even if you did bring yon young pup with you." He motioned with his head toward the front door.

Elizabeth, who had been growing to prefer Darcy's sense of playfulness to her father's sardonic humour, sighed with exasperation.

Darcy was grateful when the carriage finally pulled up in front of his townhouse. After helping Georgiana out, he strode into the house, where he was met by a flustered Philips. "Mr. Darcy!" he exclaimed. "We were not expecting you, sir."

"I apologize for failing to send notice, Philips; we left Pemberley rather unexpectedly." Darcy handed over his hat and coat.

"I will have your rooms prepared immediately, sir. Would you like some refreshment?"

"Yes, if Cook could put something together, I am sure we would all appreciate it."

"Right away, sir. And, Mr. Darcy, I should mention that Colonel Fitzwilliam has been staying here; I hope that is not a problem, sir."

"Not in the least." Darcy wondered what would have brought his cousin to town again so shortly after his last visit, as the gentleman himself appeared in the hallway to check on the commotion.

"Darcy!" Colonel Fitzwilliam exclaimed. "What brings you here?" He kissed Georgiana's cheek warmly.

"A matter of business," said Darcy briefly.

"And dare I ask how the lovely Miss Bennet is?" Colonel Fitzwilliam asked with a knowing smile.

Darcy slapped his gloves against his cousin's arm. "Lovelier than ever, and not long to bear the name of Bennet," he said good-humouredly.

The colonel raised his eyebrows. "That was quick work, Darcy. I take it the difficulties were overrated?"

"Not at all," Darcy responded with a satisfied smile. "I was merely very convincing."

"Is that so? Do I take it then that pistols at dawn are off?"

Darcy looked pleased. "Yes; I have decided to wait until you challenge me instead - then I can choose rapiers and spoil your pretty looks for you, cousin. Now, may I sit down in my own house, or are you planning an inquisition before you let us past the door?"

Colonel Fitzwilliam bowed elaborately and gestured them past him. Georgiana, after the long ride, wanted nothing so much as the opportunity to refresh herself, and proceeded to her rooms, while the gentlemen retired to the sitting room. Once they were settled, Darcy asked, "So, what are you doing here, Fitzwilliam?"

"Apart from drinking your port? Well, you know that I went back up to Newcastle, and no sooner had I arrived than his lordship sent me straight back here to indulge the Major General again, and then we repeated the whole cycle one more time, after which I told his Lordship that I thought it would be far more efficient for me to remain in London while he sent me instructions by post, rather than keeping the instructions in Newcastle and sending me back and forth by post. So, since you were away, and planning to shoot me at dawn as well, I imposed upon my dear brother and stayed with him for two days, after which I thought it unlikely that I would survive long enough for you to shoot me, so I decamped and threw myself on the mercy of Philips, who took pity upon me and took me in. He has not allowed me to drink *too* much of your port, though, more's the pity."

"Fitzwilliam, you are welcome to every last drop of my port, and the rest of the wine cellar as well," Darcy said meaningfully.

Colonel Fitzwilliam inclined his head. "Always happy to be of service. Now, what is this business that brings you post-haste to London and away from your lovely fiancée?"

Darcy grimaced. "Well, fortunately for my sanity, Elizabeth is only as far as Cheapside, but less fortunately, I have another problem with George Wickham."

"Wickham? That blackguard - what has he done now? If he has so much as looked at Georgiana...." The colonel's mien was threatening.

"No, this has nothing to do with her. He is trying the same trick again, though, but this time he has run off with Elizabeth's youngest sister. They are hiding here in town somewhere." Darcy drained his glass. "I need to find him and make him marry her."

"Is *that* all? No dragons to slay?"

"Believe me, Fitzwilliam, I would rather go up against a dragon any day. But, as it happens, it is Wickham, not a dragon, that is upsetting Elizabeth, so I go after Wickham."

"How difficult do you think it will be?"

"It will be very expensive. I doubt it will be difficult. Wickham has always known how to state his price," said Darcy sardonically.

"I take it he knows of your engagement."

"It appears so. I cannot imagine any other reason he would be interested in Lydia; the Bennets have no money, and she is hardly a prize in other ways. No, he is after me, I have no doubts."

Colonel Fitzwilliam helped himself to another glass of port. "Well, then, what do we do first?"

"We?"

"Of course. You cannot think I intend to let you have all the excitement of dealing with Wickham yourself, do you? I still have a few things to say to him about the matter of Georgiana." Colonel Fitzwilliam had no intention of letting Wickham take advantage of Darcy as he had in the past; the man was too skilled at playing on Darcy's feelings.

"He is not worth pistols at dawn, Fitzwilliam," said Darcy.

"Obviously not, and even if he were, I would never challenge him, since he would be certain to find some way to cheat."

Darcy laughed. "I appreciate the offer, but I believe that I will be able to manage him myself."

"I think it is only fair to warn you that I intend to be stubborn about this," Colonel Fitzwilliam said amiably.

"And to think that I once believed that I had some measure of control over my life! Well, I am not about to face you over a bottle of port again, so if it matters so much to you, you are welcome to join me - perhaps you can keep *me* from violence."

"Darcy!" he said with surprise. "You are becoming surprisingly reasonable. If this is the effect of Miss Bennet, I must say that she will be a fine addition to the family."

"She has taught me a few hard lessons," said Darcy, "but she is worth every one of them."

The meeting with Mr. Bennet the next morning started on a harmonious note, in part because the main participants had each resolved to make an effort to restrain their tempers, and in part because the presence of Mr. Gardiner and Colonel Fitzwilliam diffused the tension. Darcy had also managed to steal a few minutes to talk to Elizabeth beforehand, which relieved his distress over her absence while at the same time frustrating him with the limitations on their contact and conversation in this new setting.

Mr. Bennet revealed as much of the history of the elopement as was known to him, as well as the efforts which had been made to discover Wickham and Lydia, before asking Darcy for his ideas on how they might be located. After Darcy had detailed the connections whom he planned to contact in an effort to find Wickham, Colonel Fitzwilliam presented the question of import to him. "Mr. Bennet, is it certain that Wickham was aware of your daughter's engagement to Mr. Darcy?"

Mr. Bennet, like Elizabeth, had not particularly considered this connection until it was mentioned, and took a moment to reflect on it. "Lydia certainly knew of it; we had received a letter - a note, really - earlier from her mentioning it." He decided that it would be impolitic to mention that Lydia had been making sport of it at the time.

"So we must assume that Wickham knows as well," said Colonel Fitzwilliam. "The question then arises as to his motivation, which I believe that we should address before anyone actually speaks with him."

"His motivation?" asked Mr. Bennet skeptically, having not considered any possibility beyond that which any scoundrel would see in an available young woman.

"Yes, I would like to know whether he is looking for money or revenge," the colonel said. "It would affect our negotiating position."

"His primary motivation is always money," said Darcy tiredly. "Revenge is usually incidental, although it may have a higher priority this time, as I gather he was rather attached to Elizabeth at one time. He would not take kindly to her choosing me over him."

Mr. Bennet raised an eyebrow. The idea had not crossed his mind that Wickham's prior relationship with Darcy was involved, and it cast somewhat of a new light on Darcy's interest in the matter.

Colonel Fitzwilliam drummed his fingers. "Darcy, what will the effect of this affair be on your marriage plans?"

Darcy, displeased by the implication of his cousin's words, especially in front of Mr. Bennet, said shortly, "None whatsoever, as I believe you know."

"You mentioned last night that your wedding would have to be delayed until this situation was resolved."

"I would think so," interjected Mr. Bennet. "We have already postponed Jane's wedding."

"So," the colonel said thoughtfully, "Wickham essentially has the power to delay your wedding indefinitely if he refuses to negotiate. We have a potential stalemate on our hands."

At his words, Darcy dropped his head into his hands. This was not a possibility he had considered, but it was well within the range of Wickham's fertile imagination. The despondency he felt at the idea of having to wait raised an absolute sense of fury with Wickham. He pushed the feelings away. "That raises his price from expensive to exorbitant. So be it," he said, his voice carefully neutral.

Mr. Bennet looked closely at Darcy. It was beginning to come clear to him that Darcy had greater depths than he had initially thought.

"There would seem to be one other possibility," said Mr. Gardiner slowly.

"And what would that be?" Darcy asked, unable to hide his sense of hopelessness as well as he might have wished.

"You could marry Lizzy immediately. That would obviate the hold he has, I would think," Mr. Gardiner said.

"Now *that* idea has possibilities!" said Colonel Fitzwilliam, sounding pleased. "Darcy, what think you of it?"

Darcy's face became a closed mask. "It is a possibility, I suppose."

His apparent disinterest in the idea raised fears in Mr. Bennet as to the true effect of Lydia's behaviour on Darcy's intentions. "You have some objection to the idea, Mr. Darcy?" he said silkily. If Darcy were to do anything to hurt Elizabeth, Mr. Bennet was not going to be answerable for his behaviour.

Colonel Fitzwilliam's laugh rang out, breaking the tension of the moment. "You clearly do not know my cousin, sir. That is the look which says that he is fighting overwhelming temptation. I strongly suspect that he would like nothing better than to marry your daughter immediately." Darcy gave him a hostile stare, but did not argue the point.

The corners of Mr. Bennet's mouth began to twitch. Perhaps Darcy had some potential for providing amusement after all. "Well," he said mildly, "perhaps it will not be necessary. We can always reconsider the idea as the need arises."

"I would disagree," said Colonel Fitzwilliam. "Unless we act upon it now, I think we should put the idea aside completely.

It would not be a good idea to let Wickham see that he has that level of impact on Darcy's behaviour."

"And would he not know that if we rushed them to the altar now?" asked Mr. Gardiner.

"No, not necessarily. Marriage on the spur of the moment is the sort of thing that would not surprise anyone who knew Darcy well, and Wickham is certainly well acquainted with his impulsive side." At Colonel Fitzwilliam's words, Mr. Bennet and Mr. Gardiner exchanged glances; 'impulsive' and 'Darcy' were not concepts that either tended to associate together.

Darcy rolled his eyes. "Fitzwilliam, about the port and the pistols at dawn - I take it all back," he said in a quietly dangerous voice, earning a broad smile from his cousin.

"Well, perhaps I should inquire, then, as to what your objections are to the idea of immediate marriage, Mr. Darcy," said Mr. Gardiner.

Darcy looked up toward the ceiling. "I do not believe that it is the sort of wedding that Elizabeth has in mind, sir."

"Is that your only objection?"

Darcy considered the matter. "Yes," he said briefly.

Mr. Bennet drummed his fingers on the arm of his chair, watching Darcy closely. He had no particular desire to marry Elizabeth off quickly; he was dreading her eventual departure from Longbourn quite enough as it was, and he certainly was not in a hurry to bring Darcy into the family. To his mind, Darcy had been nothing but trouble since he first appeared at the Meryton assembly. Still, he had given his consent - not that there had been another alternative - and the marriage had to take place sooner or later. "Well, Mr. Darcy," he said abruptly, "I certainly appreciate your sensitivity to Lizzy's wishes. However, I must point out that I have *three* daughters who are affected by this matter, and if marrying Lizzy off immediately improves the chances for Jane's wedding to take place and Lydia's situation to be resolved, I am afraid that Lizzy will have to accept the situation."

Steepling his fingers, Darcy looked at Mr. Bennet for a moment. "I will not overrule Elizabeth's wishes in this regard," he said in an uncompromising voice.

"*I* will," said Mr. Bennet, matching tone for tone. "And I will remind you that until such a time as she actually marries you, mine is the voice she must heed. But perhaps we should speak with Lizzy; she may well be perfectly amenable to the plan if we explain the reasoning."

"*I* will speak with Elizabeth," Darcy said firmly. He could imagine her reaction to hearing that they had been determining plans for her; at least he could present it to her as a choice from his point of view. If her father chose to insist after that, Elizabeth could hardly blame him for that.

"As you wish," said Mr. Bennet, who was now convinced that Darcy would be providing him excellent entertainment for years to come.

Darcy discovered Elizabeth in the breakfast room where she was taking advantage of the excellent light to complete some fine work on her embroidery. She was also endeavoring to practice patience; she was feeling her exclusion from the discussion among the gentlemen more than she liked. She knew better than to expect to be included, but as her father's favourite in a household of women, she was more accustomed than most young women to having the opportunity of expressing her opinions. At Pemberley, Darcy had included her and Mrs. Gardiner in his planning. Elizabeth was finding her lonely relegation to marginality displeasing, and suspicions that she had best accustom herself to this position did not improve her disposition. That she missed Darcy did not help matters in the least.

Darcy's entrance lightened her mood considerably. She smiled at him, and he firmly if improperly closed the door behind him before taking her into his arms. He sought out her lips with all the pent-up need of the past two days, feeling himself restored by the taste and the feel of her as she returned his kisses. Holding her close, he allowed himself to revel in the feeling of loving her and being loved, and briefly let his cares fall away in her arms.

Elizabeth's only desire at that moment was to remain in his arms forever, but she knew that her uncle's standards for behaviour in his house were such that he would not tolerate the closed door for even a few minutes. "William, someone is bound to come in," she said breathlessly.

"No, we will be left alone; I am supposed to be convincing you of something." He trailed kisses along her jaw before returning to her mouth.

"And what is it that you are to convince me of?" she asked, her desire to resist him fading rapidly in face of the onslaught of sensation he was provoking within her.

"At the moment, I only want to convince you to kiss me again," said Darcy feelingly, wanting to preserve the sensation of Elizabeth's arms around him, especially given that he suspected that she might soon not be feeling quite so warmly toward him.

With a playful smile, she pulled his head down to hers again for a delightfully deep kiss. "You see, I am not so difficult to convince, at least when the question is the correct one," she teased.

He returned her attentions with equal fervor. "Unfortunately, you may not be as fond of the next question, my love."

Hearing the serious undertone in his voice, Elizabeth pulled back slightly, concerned as to what could make Darcy so apprehensive about her reaction. Trying to quell a sense of anxiety, she said, "Perhaps you had best ask this terrible question, then, William."

"They want us to marry immediately," he said.

Elizabeth had not known what to expect, but, anticipating that it would relate to Lydia, was taken completely by surprise. "I beg your pardon?" she asked incredulously, pulling away from him.

"Tomorrow, if possible," he said tentatively, seeing how stiff she had become. He could see that he had gone about this in the wrong way, and her look concerned him. Unhappily aware that she was displeased by the same prospect that he found eminently satisfying, he said, "I am explaining this badly; please let me try again." He briefly recounted the concerns regarding Wickham's response to their engagement and the potential for his using it against them, and why this solution had been suggested. "I told them that I would not support it unless you agreed to it," he said worriedly.

Elizabeth, able to hear the cold light of reason in the plan, softened slightly, but her heart continued to rebel at the sensation of having her choices taken away from her. Although there was a certain temptation to the idea, she did not yet feel ready to put her girlhood behind her so abruptly, to accept that she would never again return to Longbourn as her home, never again talk with Jane late into the night. She would be happy to know that she need no longer be separated from Darcy, but to think of herself so abruptly thrust into his household, under his management - she was not ready for it. She had anticipated the next month to accustom herself to the idea of moving from her father's care to her husband's, not to mention the change it would demand in her relationship with Darcy. She could see, too, that Darcy was more anxious for her answer than the situation seemed to warrant, given his words; he was indeed not skilled at disguise, and she could tell that he knew more than he had told her.

"Are you so worried, then, about what Wickham may do with this?" she asked.

"No, I.... in truth, the idea that he could make it difficult for us to marry is worrisome, but we would find some way to manage, I am sure."

"Then what is concerning you so, William?" Her suspicions were still raised.

He closed his eyes, wishing that she were slightly less perceptive. The truth was that, given Mr. Bennet's stance, he saw no choice in the matter unless they were willing to risk a major confrontation, and he desperately wanted Elizabeth to be pleased about marrying him. He could see no solution that would satisfy everyone. "I do not believe that this is what you would wish, and I do not wish to make you unhappy, yet I see conflict no matter the decision we reach. While I have said that I would not support forcing you into this arrangement, your father is not of the same opinion; he sees it as sacrificing your preferences in timing to improve the chances of both Lydia and Jane to marry, and he has said that he will insist on it."

This way of looking at it had not occurred to Elizabeth, and she wrapped her arms around herself as she forced herself to consider it. He was right; she could not be so selfish as to risk her sisters' future for her own comfort. "Very well," she said, her voice steady, but far from warm. "You have convinced me."

"Elizabeth," he said with obvious distress, "I want you to feel happy about marrying me. I do not want you to pay the price for my conflict with Wickham, for my failure to expose his actions to the world, and I feel helpless to prevent it."

The pain in his voice made her heart lurch; she feared that he was interpreting her response as a rejection of him. "I *am* happy about marrying you, William," she said gently, putting her arms around him. "This comes as a shock, that is all; I admit that

I do not feel quite ready for this step, but I have faith that you and I will find a way to make it work."

"Dearest Elizabeth," he said, relief apparent in his voice. "I will do anything in my power to make you happy." He kissed her lightly, his mind travelling to the possibility that she would be his soon, and his body's response to the thought was undeniable. Between his anticipation and his fear of her rejection, he could feel his possessive need for her about to spiral out of his control, and he disentangled himself from her gently, keeping only her hands in his. As he raised them to his lips, he asked, his eyes beseeching, "Are you certain, my love?"

"I am quite certain," she said steadily, looking into his eyes as she saw his need for reassurance. "Are the details settled? I would like to know the plans."

"Not as of yet; perhaps we should join the others to discuss that now," he said, concerned by the idea of leaving her alone with her thoughts.

She smiled at him warmly, pleased that he would include her. "Yes, let us do that."

He was still not completely reassured, and with an effort forced himself to make an offer that went against his deepest wishes. "Elizabeth, I do realize that this is rushing you, and I want to say that I .... I will not ask anything of you that you are not ready to give."

Her face took on an affectionate look of amusement. "William, you do worry about the most unlikely things sometimes." She was relieved to see his slight smile in response to her words, and accepted a kiss whose intimacy clearly held promises for the future.

He led her back to the study, where the other three gentlemen were deep in conversation which abruptly ceased on their entrance. Mr. Bennet raised an eyebrow at the sight of his daughter. "Well, Lizzy?" he enquired.

"I have given my consent," she said, receiving a grateful look from Darcy.

"Excellent!" said Colonel Fitzwilliam. "We have been making plans in your absence, Darcy, and have determined that your task for today is to get the license. I will speak with the rector at St. George's - I assume you do want St. George's, Darcy? - and Mr. Gardiner will try to obtain further information as to the present location of Mrs. Yonge and Wickham's other London friends."

"My task," said Mr. Bennet dryly, "is to remain here and be useless. It seems that I am not to be trusted with any of these negotiations."

"You are too close to the concerns, brother," said Mr. Gardiner. "I can be more detached."

"I should warn you, Mr. Darcy, that you have been equally dispossessed; these gentlemen have determined that you cannot be trusted to deal directly with Wickham either," said Mr. Bennet, watching with some amusement to see his reaction to this intelligence.

He was not disappointed. Darcy's face darkened as he said, "Dealing with Wickham is my responsibility, mine and no other's. It is my fault that his character has not been exposed before this, and it stands with me to remedy it."

Colonel Fitzwilliam was prepared for this response. "No one is trying to take away your part in this - we are just suggesting that you are not the ideal negotiator if our goal is resolution of the situation. First of all, he knows you well enough to manipulate you, Darcy, and second, I do not trust your temper at the moment. Wickham knows that I would just as soon run him through as not, and hopefully that will keep his demands within reason. You will have your turn with him soon enough, cousin."

"We will discuss this *later*, Fitzwilliam," said Darcy grimly, more than willing to take out his anger over causing Elizabeth distress on his cousin.

"As you wish," said Colonel Fitzwilliam with a shrug, clearly not at all concerned by the concept.

Elizabeth had expressed a desire to visit Georgiana, so after the gentlemen had departed on their various tasks, she convinced her father to escort her to the Darcy townhouse. She was pleased to discover that it was only a few houses away from Hyde Park, ideal for her favoured walks.

Georgiana was delighted to see her, and took Elizabeth and Mr. Bennet on a tour of the main rooms of the house. It was not a surprise to find that it was as elegantly appointed as Pemberley, although in a more fashionable style. Elizabeth's pulses fluttered a bit at the thought that it would become her home tomorrow, and she coloured as certain implications of that came to her mind.

Georgiana seemed to think that the news of an immediate wedding was a cause for excitement rather than concern. After her first raptures were over, she announced that there was no choice but to visit the milliner immediately to purchase new gloves and a new bonnet for Elizabeth for the occasion, although she acknowledged with a sigh that unfortunately there would be insufficient time to have a new dress made. Elizabeth initially demurred, saying that what she already had would serve well enough, but after noticing how animated the prospect of a shopping trip made Georgiana, who had been very quiet since the news of Lydia and Wickham, she reconsidered and accepted the offer.

"I must admit, though, that I have no idea where one goes in town for such things," confessed Elizabeth.

"Oh, that is no problem," Georgiana said eagerly. "We can go to the my milliner, and if she has nothing appropriate, I know that she will help us find something. I like her very much; she has lovely things."

Elizabeth laughingly agreed to the proposal. Mr. Bennet, feeling that his time could be more profitably spent exploring Darcy's library than discussing lace, opted not to join them.

Once at the milliner's shop, which obviously catered to a wealthier clientele than the shops she had patronized with her aunt, it became clear that shopping was one setting in which shyness did not affect Georgiana. She seemed well-known there, and when she introduced Elizabeth as Darcy's intended, the staff were very excited by the intelligence. It was not until she purchased new gloves, a new bonnet, and several other items of a far higher quality than that to which she was accustomed that Georgiana was satisfied. Elizabeth instructed the shopkeeper to send the bill to her father at Gracechurch Street, but Georgiana overruled her and had it all placed on the Darcy account, much to Elizabeth's discomfort. She was acutely aware of how much the situation with Wickham was likely to cost Darcy, and she hardly wished to spend any more of his money at the moment. Georgiana then insisted that they visit a modiste to examine patterns and fabrics as well in preparation for ordering new dresses, but Elizabeth, cognizant of the cost of this adventure, laughingly put her off.

"You will need to do it soon in any case," said Georgiana winningly. "We could at least see what is available." Elizabeth eventually allowed herself to be persuaded with the agreement that there would be no further purchases, but by the time they had viewed many fabrics and models, Georgiana was not to be gainsaid, and insisted on ordering one new dress for Elizabeth.

On the way back to Brook Street, Georgiana took the opportunity to point out some of her favourite shops, as well as taking Elizabeth past Grosvenor Square and through the neighborhood. Elizabeth was still bemused by the transformation in her when they returned to the house to find Mr. Bennet and Mr. Darcy looking daggers at one another over glasses of port.

Darcy's face warmed gratifyingly when he saw her; he had been successful in obtaining the license, and was feeling quite ready to join her life to his. Seeing her come back to *his* house after what had clearly been a pleasant outing with *his* sister was a fine reminder of how pleasant it would be when she was his wife.

Elizabeth raised an eyebrow at her father when she noticed the tension in the room. She was tolerably well acquainted with how her father's behaviour affected Darcy, but she was not completely certain to what extent her father chose to quarrel with him over actual concerns rather than for his own amusement. "Mr. Darcy," she said lightly. "You had not warned me of the dangers of shopping with your sister. I fear that despite my best efforts she has been attempting to bankrupt you."

"I am sure it is in a good cause," he said affectionately, kissing her hand.

"Well," said Mr. Bennet abruptly, "It is time for us to be returning to your uncle's house, Lizzy."

Darcy rolled his eyes upward. "If I may beg a minute's indulgence, sir, there is something which I would like to show to Elizabeth." The tension in his voice belied his polite words.

"As you wish, Mr. Darcy." Mr. Bennet's eyes followed them as Darcy led Elizabeth from the room.

He showed her into his study and let out a pent-up breath. "Elizabeth, I am beginning to think that your father positively delights in annoying me."

She kissed him lightly. "It is quite possible; I cannot think why else he should be so harsh with you."

He took her into his arms, thinking that he himself might well not be too fond of the man who would take Georgiana away from him. "As long as it does not affect how *you* feel, my love, I can tolerate it. But I did not bring you here to talk about your father, or even to kiss you, though that is a very appealing idea."

With an amused smile, Elizabeth took his hint and put her arms around his neck and offered him her lips. It was several pleasant minutes before she pulled away from him and said, "There was something you wished to speak to me about, I believe?"

He laughed softly. "I have something to give you, in fact. I brought this with me from Pemberley, thinking that I might not have the chance to return there before we married, though I did not anticipate that it would be quite so soon as this! It would please me if you wore this tomorrow." He drew a long box out of a drawer of his desk. He handed it to her, and when she looked questioningly at him, said, "It is yours, my love. Open it."

Raising the lid, she gasped as the sight of a diamond and sapphire necklace, obviously an heirloom, and exquisite in its simplicity. Speechless, she touched it lightly with one finger, and then looked up to find a pleased smile on Darcy's face. "William, I ... I hardly know what to say." She had never received such an extravagant gift - nor even dreamed of receiving one - and did not even know how to express her thanks.

"It belonged to my mother. Most of her jewels are Georgiana's, but she left me this to give to my wife. It matches the ring I gave you," he said somewhat shyly.

She looked up at him, thinking of how much he enjoyed giving Georgiana gifts, and recognizing he likely would derive the same enjoyment with her. "Thank you, William," she said, feeling words were inadequate. "I shall be proud to wear it."

He lifted it out of its case, and placed it around her neck, then stepped back to admire the sight. He had long pictured her wearing it; since he associated it so strongly with the woman he would marry, it was almost a badge of possession in his mind. He smiled, thinking of her wearing it after they were married, when he would have the right to have her always beside him.

Seeing the warmth of his look, Elizabeth slipped her arms around his neck and kissed him, a gesture which he returned and deepened. She sighed happily as he clasped her to him, and set to enjoy the taste of his lips, stirred by feeling his strong body against hers. When they paused for breath, she said, "I do love you so."

Deeply aroused, he murmured, "My dearest Elizabeth," as his hands began to explore the curves of her back. One day suddenly seemed a very long time to wait before making her his, and he could not resist taking advantage of her obvious response to press kisses down her neck in the way that he knew to stimulate her.

His sudden passion and evocative touch left her feeling weak, and she impulsively slipped her hands inside his tailcoat, enjoying feeling the warmth of his chest and shoulders. Her act provoked a clear reaction in him, and he pressed against her while seeking her mouth demandingly. "William, love," she whispered against his lips, feeling her entire body craving more of him.

Darcy was struggling to convince himself to stop with kisses when such a tempting range of delights was before him, and eventually found the strength to call a halt to his demands of her. He leaned his forehead against hers, and said huskily, "You are the only woman in the world for me, my love."

His words touched her deeply, and as she worked to calm herself, the thought came to her that the next time this occurred, there would be no need to stop. This reflection was at the same time gratifying and anxiety-provoking, and she sought to push it from her mind as quickly as possible.

"Your father will have yet one more item to hold against me if I do not return you to him soon," said Darcy, who was beginning to question his ability to restrain himself if she remained in his arms any longer.

She released him and stepped back with a smile. "We cannot have that, can we?"

He stroked a finger down her cheek lightly. "Tomorrow, Elizabeth," he said, his words a promise.

She tried to swallow the morsel of fear that came to her. "Tomorrow," she echoed, gazing into his eyes.

"You and Mr. Darcy seem to be developing an interesting relationship," said Elizabeth to Mr. Bennet as they were travelling back to Gracechurch Street.

"Hmm. By that I take it that you mean that we quarrel quite readily, Lizzy," said Mr. Bennet mildly.

Elizabeth considered this. "No more than two cornered tomcats, but yes, you do seem to have your moments."

"He is a very serious fellow, your Mr. Darcy."

"Until he knows you well, that is perhaps true."

"He is very easy to provoke, especially on the subject of you, Lizzy."

"And you delight in provoking him, do you not?" she challenged him.

"He is taking my last chance for intelligent conversation far away from Longbourn and leaving me to the mercies of your mother, Mary, and Kitty," he said. "The least he deserves for that is a little provocation, I would say. I could wish that you had found yourself a young man a little closer to home, Lizzy."

"I hope that you will visit us at Pemberley often. We will be happy to provide sensible conversation, at least if you and Mr. Darcy can manage to keep the peace for more than a few minutes at a time."

Mr. Bennet patted her hand. "Never fear, Lizzy, I am sure that we will manage somehow. It is never easy for a father to admit that another man has won his daughter's allegiance, and I do not doubt that it is hard for Mr. Darcy to accept that you owe allegiance to anyone but him."

Elizabeth smiled at this characterization of her admittedly possessive fiancé. "You object to him harbouring strong feelings for me?" she asked pointedly.

"Enough, Lizzy! I shall endeavour to be kind to your Mr. Darcy, if it will earn me peace!"

Elizabeth laughed, well pleased with this resolution.

Elizabeth slept fitfully that night and awoke early, her thoughts immediately flying to the day ahead. She found herself surprisingly anxious, and she dearly wished that Jane were with her, or at least her aunt. Jane would be able to reassure her, to remind her that Darcy loved her, and that this was what she herself wanted, even if the circumstances were somewhat lacking. She fidgeted until the maid arrived to help her dress.

In the breakfast room she found that none of the foods appealed, but forced herself to choose something to fortify herself for what was to come. Her father joined her, looking to be in far from the best of spirits himself; Elizabeth had to remind herself that his mind was also very much preoccupied with Lydia's situation, and that her wedding was not his only priority. He roused himself sufficiently to tease her about Darcy, but her usual sense of the ridiculous seemed to have deserted her for once, and she felt only mild irritation.

She found it hard to settle herself after breakfast, and was glad when it came time to dress for the wedding. The maid helped her into the one formal gown she had brought on the journey to Derbyshire for the contingency of calling on Lord and Lady Matlock; she had hardly thought to marry in it. She found herself again wishing for Jane to share these moments with her - it was hard to feel celebratory all alone. The maid was just finishing her hair when Mrs. Harper, the housekeeper, made an entrance.

Elizabeth greeted her with a smile. Over the years that she had visited with the Gardiners, Mrs. Harper had been a motherly presence who always had a few moments to spoil the young Jane and Elizabeth. She gave Elizabeth her best wishes on the day, and shooed the maid out.

She handed Elizabeth her bonnet and gloves. "You have quite a day ahead of you, Miss Elizabeth," she said.

Grateful for any companionship at this juncture, Elizabeth agreed, thanking her for her wishes.

"It happened to occur to me," said Mrs. Harper as she helped to smooth the new gloves on Elizabeth's arm, "that it happens that neither your aunt nor your mother are here with you today, and that, since you weren't to be expecting this to take place, it might be that neither of them had talked to you about it yet."

"Only in generalities." Elizabeth wondered at the housekeeper's intent.

"It also happened to occur to me - and begging your pardon, Miss Elizabeth - that Mrs. Gardiner would never forgive me if I were to let you go to your marriage bed as ignorant as the day you were born. She doesn't hold with such notions, no indeed."

Elizabeth smiled even as the colour rose in her cheeks. Yes, her aunt would indeed not hold with such notions, she knew, but what she would have thought of Elizabeth learning the facts from the housekeeper was more of a question. She certainly did not want to admit to Mrs. Harper that she had discovered a bit more of it than she was supposed to have done, but, in fact, the question of what was to come had been on her mind. She thanked Mrs. Harper for her consideration, and listened carefully if somewhat nervously to her explanations.

The housekeeper concluded by saying, "If your man is a kind one, and he cares for you, it should be a happy experience for you. If he cares only for his own pleasure, then perhaps not." She hooked the sapphire necklace around Elizabeth's neck, and looked her over from head to foot. "There. You will do very nicely, Miss Elizabeth."

Elizabeth devoutly hoped she was correct.

Colonel Fitzwilliam was waiting in the portico of the church for the bride's party to arrive when an elegant carriage pulled up and disgorged his brother and his wife. The newcomer advanced on the Colonel with a displeased look in his eyes, and said, "What am I to make of this, Richard? *'Meet me at St. George's, eleven o'clock tomorrow, bring family, urgent?'* What game is this?"

"It is a pleasure to see you, too, Edward," replied the Colonel amiably. "I thought that you might want to see Darcy wed, so I invited you."

"Darcy? Married? He is not even engaged!" snapped the Viscount irritably.

Colonel Fitzwilliam held up his hands. "I am not to blame if he chooses not to tell you these things!"

"Are you *quite* serious, Colonel?" asked Lady Langley.

"*Quite* serious," he assured her.

"Then perhaps we should go in," she suggested to her husband, who acquiesced with a scowl.

Mr. Bennet, Mr. Gardiner, and Elizabeth were next to arrive, and Colonel Fitzwilliam was able to explain the arrangements for the service to them without further ado. He was about to return inside to Darcy when he noticed the strained look on Elizabeth's face. He took a moment to go to her side and said quietly, "Miss Bennet, you are about to marry a good man who loves you more than life itself. There is no cause for worry."

She smiled at him, grateful for his concern for her feelings. "I do know that, sir. It is just that it is quite a change for me," she said. *And I, like a lost child, am frantically wishing that my family were here,* she thought. It was an unusual day indeed that found her missing her mother.

"All will be well," he said warmly. "I shall see you inside."

A few minutes later, Elizabeth felt a profound sense of unreality as she walked down the aisle of the unfamiliar church on her father's arm. The sense that she was leaving her world to move into Darcy's was an alarming one. It felt an impossibly long way to the altar, and her heart pounded as she walked. When she finally stood beside Darcy at the altar she took a deep breath to quell her dizziness, then looked up at him. The look of warmth in his dark eyes comforted her as the minister began to speak.

Darcy, who had been waiting eagerly to see Elizabeth, was immediately concerned by her pallor, and felt half an impulse to stop the service to see if she needed assistance. His first thought, that she did not want to marry him, he recognized to be an unreasonable fear; the way she looked at him told him that it was not true, and it occurred to him that he was not sure that he had ever seen Elizabeth frightened in the time he had known her. He wished that he could take her in his arms and restore the roses to her cheeks. He realized with a shock that he had not been paying the slightest attention to the minister's words, and that he was reaching a point where his response was required.

"Wilt thou have this woman to thy wedded wife, to live together after God's ordinance in the holy estate of matrimony? Wilt thou love her, comfort her, honour, and keep her in sickness and in health; and, forsaking all other, keep thee only unto her, so long as ye both shall live?" the minister recited.

Darcy looked at Elizabeth, willing her to meet his eyes as he responded, "I will." He was relieved to see her normal colour returning, and he kept his gaze locked with hers as the service continued.

"Wilt thou have this man to thy wedded husband, to live together after God's ordinance in the holy estate of matrimony? Wilt thou obey him, and serve him, love, honour, and keep him in sickness and in health; and, forsaking all other, keep thee only unto him, so long as ye both shall live?"

Elizabeth, who had heard even less of the service than Darcy, was able to manage a small smile as she said quietly, "I will."

"Who giveth this woman to be married to this man?"

Mr. Bennet kissed her cheek before releasing her, a suspicious sheen in his eyes. As Darcy took her hand, the warmth of his hand was a lifeline to her, and abruptly everything seemed real to her again. Her fingers tightened on his, and as he returned the pressure, she was reminded of the very first time he had taken her hand in the curricle while driving her back to Longbourn, and an affectionate smile crossed her face. Suddenly she was glad to be there, glad to be marrying him.

His face lightened as he saw her obvious relief, even if he could not understand it. His intense gaze fixed on her as he repeated the words of his vows, "I, Fitzwilliam, take thee, Elizabeth, to my wedded wife, to have and to hold from this day forward, for better for worse, for richer for poorer, in sickness and in health, to love and to cherish, till death us do part, according to God's holy ordinance; and thereto I plight thee my troth."

Elizabeth's voice was stronger than it had been earlier as she in turn took him as her husband and promised to love, cherish, and to obey him. The light of the smile dawning on Darcy's face could not be denied as he slid the ring onto her finger and said in a voice rich with meaning, "With this ring I thee wed, with my body I thee worship, and with all my worldly goods

I thee endow: in the name of the Father, and of the Son, and of the Holy Ghost. Amen."

As they knelt for the prayer, Elizabeth realized that it no longer mattered to her that the marriage had been rushed, that her family was far away; all that mattered was the man at her side. The minister joined their hands again, and said the words over them, "Those whom God hath joined together let no man put asunder."

*It is done*, thought Darcy. *After all this time, after all the pain, it is done.* He looked down at the ring on her finger, and wished fervently that the rest of the world would disappear, leaving him alone with her. But his wishes were not to be granted; once the service was over, he knew they would have to accept congratulations from their family members, and then go home with Georgiana and Colonel Fitzwilliam. He would not be alone with Elizabeth until they retired for the night, which at that moment seemed years away.

As they walked together back down the aisle, he whispered, "You looked pale earlier. Is all well, Mrs. Darcy?"

She smiled at him, and he saw that sparkle that he loved so in her eyes as she said, "I am very well indeed, Mr. Darcy, though I shall never again laugh at a case of bridal nerves!"

"I adore you," he said in her ear just before the others joined them.

Colonel Fitzwilliam offered them his heartiest congratulations. "Mrs. Darcy, may I present my brother, Lord Langley, and his wife, Lady Langley? Mrs. Darcy is the former Miss Elizabeth Bennet, Edward."

Elizabeth greeted Viscount Langley, a thin man with a look of chronic dyspepsia. Lady Langley was dressed in an elegant fashion which quite outshone Elizabeth's country best, a fact which she had clearly noted. Elizabeth hid a smile. It was hard to imagine the amiable Colonel Fitzwilliam coming from the same stock as his brother.

"Bennet - I do not believe that I have heard that name before," said Lady Langley, managing to delicately imply that there was something quite dubious about this.

"My family is from Hertfordshire, Lady Langley, and I would hardly imagine it would come to the attention of the *ton*," said Elizabeth with a pleasant smile. Darcy put his hand over hers as if to reassure her.

Mr. Bennet and Mr. Gardiner joined them, and further introductions were made. Lady Langley's condescending attitude to her father irritated Elizabeth, and she could see that it made Darcy no more comfortable than she.

"And where is the rest of your family today, Mrs. Darcy?" asked Lord Langley.

Elizabeth, unable to resist, looked to one side of her and then the other, as if expecting to find her family. "I regret to say that I seem to have misplaced them, Lord Langley," she said. Out of the corner of her eye, she could see Darcy struggling to suppress a smile.

Colonel Fitzwilliam coughed. "Well, I must be off - I promised to spend the remainder of the day with the Major General. Edward, did you say that you were planning to invite Georgiana to dine with you? That was a kind thought; I am sure she would find Brook Street dull this afternoon."

"I said nothing of the sort!" snapped Lord Langley, who then discovered himself to be the recipient of a look from his brother that would have melted iron. "Oh, of course. Georgiana, will you be so kind as to dine with us today?" His voice was unenthusiastic.

"Thank you, that would be lovely," said Georgiana in a voice just above a whisper.

Elizabeth, although concerned for Georgiana in such company, gave Colonel Fitzwilliam a grateful glance for taking the trouble to ensure their privacy on their wedding day.

When they finally arrived back at the Darcy townhouse, they were greeted by the entire staff, lined up to meet Mrs. Darcy and to give the master their felicitations. Elizabeth did her best to try to learn names and faces, though afterward it would seem somewhat of a blur to her. The staff, apparently warned by Colonel Fitzwilliam as to his plans, had laid on an elegant luncheon for the new couple for which Elizabeth expressed her appreciation while noticing that Darcy, who had reached the point of little tolerance for other people, was becoming quite silent. It was not until after the footmen had cleared away the last of the meal they were left quite alone.

Darcy breathed a sigh of relief. "Sometimes I think that there are far too many people in the world," he said to Elizabeth's amusement.

"I fear that is part of the price of being a pillar of society."

Reaching over to take her hand, he drew her onto his lap, where she settled in with a happy sigh. Cradling her in his arms, he gave her an exploratory kiss which sent tingles of excitement through her as she inevitably thought of what was to come that night. "I am glad to have you to myself finally," he admitted, trying to find a way to raise the subject of that morning which still concerned him. Although she no longer seemed to be upset, she obviously had been earlier, and he was gradually learning the danger of being unaware of Elizabeth's thoughts and concerns. Finally he decided in favor of straightforwardness, and said, "You worried me earlier - you were so pale at the church, my love."

Elizabeth coloured. "I feel quite foolish about it. I fear that I had worked myself up to a set of nerves which would not disgrace my mother, and all over a rather silly matter."

"And what was the matter that you find silly, dearest?" he prompted.

"You will not laugh? I was panicked over being alone; I missed having Jane with me, or my aunt, and by the time I reached the church I would have settled for my mother or Mary! Somehow having my father there did not provide the reassurance that I would have found in having another woman with me. There - I told you it was foolish; I know that there were excellent reasons for marrying now, and that the most important part is being married, not who was present at the wedding."

He wondered guiltily if he should have refused to compromise on the wedding date. "My dearest love, what could be more natural than to want your family around you on your wedding day? I am so sorry that you did not; I wish that we could have had the wedding you would have liked, and I know it is because of me that it had to be this way. And, while I cannot complain of being displeased with the result --" he paused to kiss her lingeringly, and ran a finger down her neck until his hand rested lightly on her exposed shoulder, "I would have rather waited and married as you had wished."

The touch of his hand created an exquisite sense of warmth in her, and she wondered distractedly how such a slight contact could be felt throughout her. Her lips began to tingle with anticipation, and she had to force herself to concentrate on the conversation. "Had we waited, I would no doubt be complaining of how irritating my family was, and how I wished we could have married without any of them! No, William, I am simply difficult to please, and it certainly is *not* because of you that we married now; Wickham and Lydia must bear the entire brunt of that burden." Her mouth felt suddenly dry.

He saw a delightful flush rising in her cheeks, and experimentally let his thumb explore her neck, his hand otherwise remaining in place. "I am only grateful, my loveliest Elizabeth, that we need no longer be parted. I must confess that I was finding it a difficult adjustment having you halfway across the city after being with you at Pemberley. I had become quite accustomed to having you nearby." The look on her face and the feeling of her in his arms was beginning to wreak havoc on his sensibilities, and his awareness of her arousal made it increasingly difficult to consider waiting until the night.

Feeling that her entire being was concentrated in those few inches of skin that he was caressing so lightly, she found her eyes drifting to his lips, which looked so tempting that she could not help but to run her fingers along them. She heard his indrawn breath, and felt a shock of sensation as he took her finger into his mouth, catching it lightly between his teeth and running his tongue along the tip. She felt barely able to control her response; her entire body seemed to be demanding something more, and her susceptibility to him was rising as each minute went by. *How can he possibly induce such feelings in me?* she wondered with a degree of desperation. *This has to stop, or I will be reduced to begging him to take me, and it is a very long time until we retire!*

His desire for her was mounting by the minute, intensified by her look of longing, and as she closed her eyes, moving her body against his, he knew that delaying the inevitable was rapidly becoming beyond him. His thoughts began to drift ahead to what lay before them, and before he knew it he had released her finger to take hungry possession of her mouth. Beyond the realm of thought, she whispered yearningly, "Oh, William, my love."

The imploring sound of his name on her lips was more than he could bear, and he shifted his arms under her. "Elizabeth, dearest, loveliest Elizabeth," he breathed as he tasted the tender skin of her neck. "I can wait no longer." He stood with her in his arms, his heart pounding as he realized that she was making no protest, but rather held herself as close as possible to him as he carried her to the stairs. She was his wife, and she was his for the taking, and he could not imagine anything more glorious in the universe.

Afterwards Elizabeth lay in Darcy's arms, her head resting intimately on his shoulder, a slight smile upon her lips. He tangled his hand in her long curls, enjoying the pleasure of her presence beside him, and the knowledge that she was finally his. He had waited so long for this, had dreamed of it and despaired of it, and now she was in truth his wife, and apparently content to be so. He had found in her all the passion that he could have wished for, and he knew that he would be grateful for the rest of his days to have her at his side.

He was not inexperienced, but he had never known that lovemaking could be like this; that it could touch him so deeply and leave him feeling so completely accepted and yet vulnerable at the same moment. His gratitude for her love was profound, and he felt completed in a way he could never have understood in the past, and it seemed to open a capacity for happiness that was new to his experience. "Elizabeth, my most beloved Elizabeth," he murmured, only half conscious that he was speaking aloud.

Elizabeth, feeling a sense of peace and contentment unusual to her high spirits, put her hand to his cheek. He had been a gentle and thoughtful lover, and had raised her to heights of excitement and fulfilment she had never dreamed existed. She felt astonished at the feelings he had created in her, and she knew instinctively that he now knew and possessed a part of her that no one else ever would. She said softly, "I love you so, William," the words she found so difficult to say at other times coming fluently to her lips at this intimate moment.

He smiled gently. "I will always be yours," he said, holding her as if he would never let her go. Concerned, however, for her experience, he asked tenderly, "Is everything well, my love?"

She nestled closer to him, kissing his chin lightly, feeling that words could not do justice to how she felt at that moment. "Nothing could be better, nothing at all, William."

He smiled warmly at her. "I am glad to hear it, my wife," he said. Her heart raced a little at the appellation that was still so new to her as he caught her mouth with his for an intimate kiss. "I wish we could tell Georgiana and Fitzwilliam to stay away for a week."

She opened her eyes wide with a mocking look of innocence. "Only a week, my husband?"

"I think, my dearest love, that it may take years to satisfy me," he said, easing her off his shoulder so that he could prop himself up beside her. "Many years indeed." Gazing into her eyes, he caressed her cheek tenderly. "I do have a great deal of time to make up for, you know."

She ran a finger lightly down his chest. "Then you had best start working at it now."

A slow smile dawned on his face, and he answered her in the only way possible.

Author's Note: This story is an excerpt from a longer work, *The Rule of Reason*, which is not formally published owing to its overlap with *Impulse & Initiative*. If you would read more of *The Rule of Reason*, you can find it www.lulu.com.

# The Most Natural Thing

## A Novella in 3 parts

*This is a writing challenge story, dating from a time when 'Dark Darcy' stories were popular in the on-line Austen fan fiction community. I don't see Darcy as a dark character, so I decided to see what would happen if I put my Mr. Darcy in the shoes of the 'Dark Darcy,' with a golden opportunity to take advantage of Elizabeth Bennet's misfortunes. This novella is in three parts. The first was the original story I wrote, and the other parts came years later when my Muse insisted that there was more to the story.*

### Part I

"SIR, THERE IS A Miss Bennet to see you." Simms' tone expressed his dubious opinion of any young lady who would call on his master. "Shall I tell her you are out?"

It was a moment before Darcy was able to make sense of the butler's words, and even then he doubted his ears. "Did you say Miss Bennet?" He could barely bring himself to pronounce the words. "Miss *Elizabeth* Bennet?"

"She did not give her name, sir, nor did she provide a card." Simms sniffed in disapproval.

It could not be Elizabeth. What more could she possibly have to say to him after her cold words at Hunsford not a fortnight past? It would make more sense for it to be Miss Jane Bennet, pleading for another chance with Mr. Bingley, but he could not imagine her behaving with such impropriety as to call upon a single gentleman. He could imagine Elizabeth breaking such rules, but why?

There could only be one reason. She must have told her mother of his proposal, and been instructed to change her tune. Well, it was far too late for that. He would prove to her he was not a fool to be played upon. "Show her in," he said brusquely. He took a bracing gulp from the half-empty glass of port beside him and straightened his cravat, hoping the room's dim light would disguise his weary features. It would not do to have her know he had been pining over her. In truth, he had been pining over a fantasy.

Almost involuntarily he stood at the sound of her light footsteps, even before her all-too-familiar form slipped in the door. He acknowledged her with a bare nod of his head and silently gestured to a chair. He forced himself to examine her critically, noting the flaws in her complexion and the asymmetry of her form in an ill-fitting dark dress, avoiding those deep, deceptive eyes.

She sat, folding and unfolding her hands in her lap. He felt no inclination to make this easy for her, so he said nothing, though the scent of lavender that drifted across to him made him slightly dizzy.

Finally she took a deep breath. "Thank you for receiving me. I apologize for the imposition, which I would not have made were my circumstances any less desperate."

Desperate? He had not expected such melodrama from Elizabeth, but perhaps it was all part of the plan to make him compromise her and be forced to marry her. She had compromised herself enough coming here by herself; he wondered if she considered the extent to which he could ruin her reputation with a word. But even so, he felt a fleeting temptation to go along with her scheme, but then her insulting words at Hunsford rang in his ears again. She did not deserve any recognition from him. "Desperate, Miss Bennet?" he said with cold irony.

For a moment her eyes flamed, then, to his surprise, the fire was banked. Something had quelled her spirit. He wondered what punishment her mother had inflicted upon her to make her throw herself on the last man in the world she could be prevailed upon to marry. The memory of her angry countenance as she had spat those words at him made his spine stiffen.

"I am here to beg your assistance, although I have given you no reason to grant it. I should preface my request with an apology for the unfair things I said to you owing to my foolish misapprehension of Mr. Wickham, but I doubt you are in any mood to hear it, so I will come directly to my point. I have already paid bitterly for my mistaken impression of him. My family's circumstances have changed dramatically since we last met, owing to Mr. Wickham. My youngest sister, in her foolish ignorance, has run off with him. You know him too well to doubt the outcome. She has nothing to tempt him, and I fear she is lost forever."

The one appeal he had not expected, and the one he could not refuse. Still, he would not weaken, nor allow her to guess anything of the power she still held over him, despite everything she had said and done. "I am sorry to hear it. What has your father done to remedy the situation?"

"My father…." Her voice caught, and her eyes dropped. "My father will never again remedy any situation, which brings me to my request. You, sir, have great influence with my cousin, Mr. Collins. He has already taken possession of Longbourn, which was left to him under entail, and once he heard of Lydia's circumstances, he refused to allow my mother and other sisters to remain there. They are staying with relatives for the moment, but that situation cannot continue. I would ask you to use your influence to convince Mr. Collins to allow my family to return, perhaps to a cottage on the estate. Nothing can be done for my poor sister Lydia, but if you could find it in your heart to intercede on behalf of my family, I would be grateful. Beyond grateful."

There, she had said it. Elizabeth waited, her heart cold in her chest, for his response. He was her last hope, and she could only hope that his interest in her had not waned so much as to refuse this opportunity.

"On your own behalf as well, if you are to live with your family."

The candle on his desk hissed and sputtered, sending off an acrid trail of smoke. She swallowed hard. He was going to make her say it. Well, she had fallen this far, and the words made no difference in any case. Mustering her courage, she met his haughty eyes. "Not on my own behalf. I will not be returning to my family. I ceded that option when I came to you."

Not a flicker of expression crossed his face. She had expected a look of triumph, at least, at the knowledge that the proposals which she had proudly spurned only two weeks ago, would now have been gladly and gratefully received. She had hoped he would be generous in his victory. How quickly her life had changed! From refusing to be his wife, to offering him her virtue in exchange for her family's safety. It was the only currency she had, so there was no choice. What did her dignity matter now?

Faced with his stony silence, she said, "I believe it is the mode in such circumstances for the lady to smile sweetly and flutter her eyelashes in an appealing manner, but I fear it is beyond me at the moment. However, I promise to show you respect in all ways."

His mouth twisted. "Go home, Miss Bennet. I will see what I can do."

Elizabeth spent the next few days in sick anticipation, unsure whether Mr. Darcy would aid her or leave her to her fate. Oh, how she wished she had been more moderate in her speech when she had refused his proposal! She would pay for the rest of her life for her prideful errors.

The waiting and not knowing was the worst. She was surprised Mr. Darcy had not availed himself of her offer immediately. From the novels she had read, she had assumed men had little self-control in these matters. But Mr. Darcy was nothing if not self-controlled, and she supposed it was in character for him to keep his part of the bargain before demanding his payment. At least he had not taken advantage of her and then dismissed her without assistance. It would have been within his power, but she thought from his letter that he was not that sort of man. If he agreed to a bargain, he would keep it.

She was frightened by what was to come. Under the circumstances, she could not ask her aunt what to expect, as she might have were this to be a wedding, rather than a fall from grace. Soon she and Lydia would be in the same position, but at least in her case she would have the comfort of knowing her family was safe because of her actions.

A commotion in the front hall caught her attention. Could that be Lydia's voice she heard? She caught up her skirts and hurried down, only to discover the completely unanticipated sight of her sister on Wickham's arm, laughing with her aunt. Despite everything, Elizabeth felt a rush of relief at the knowledge that her sister was safe.

"Lydia!" she cried.

Lydia laughed. "No, Lizzy, now I am Mrs. Wickham! We were wed this morning!" She held out her hand, displaying a narrow gold band.

"Married?" Elizabeth's mouth was dry. She had been so certain that Lydia was lost forever, that Wickham would never marry her, but she had been wrong yet again. Why, oh, why had Lydia not been in communication with them? Had she known, she would never have had to go to Mr. Darcy and make her bargain with the devil. But now it was too late. She doubted he would release her, and her reputation was completely within his power.

Elizabeth lifted her chin. If this was to be her fate, she would meet it with courage. She would not to think of what Lydia's impulsiveness had cost her. Lydia would suffer eventually in turn, as Elizabeth was certain that Wickham's smiles and charm would fade soon enough and his true character would emerge. He was the true source of her misery. Lydia had been wild and thoughtless, but Wickham must have known the pain this would cause the Bennet family.

Suddenly she could not stand to see Lydia flaunting her happiness. "You will have to change your wedding finery for black now. Our father is dead."

The silence this comment produced was complete. Even Lydia sounded subdued when she finally broke it and said, "I did not know."

"Now you do. It would have been appreciated if you had told us about the wedding in advance. It would have saved much grief."

Lydia's eyes filled with tears. "I wanted to tell you! I wanted to invite my aunt and uncle, but Mr. Darcy said no, that the wedding must take place immediately." She clapped her hand to her mouth. "Oh, I should not have said that! I promised faithfully not to mention him."

Cold pierced her heart. Elizabeth could not bear it. She excused herself shakily and ran back to her room. They would think her grief was for her father, and it was best to leave it so. She needed to be alone to consider what she had just learned.

Mr. Darcy would never have voluntarily involved himself with Wickham, of that much she was certain. If he was there, it was for another reason. He must have made the match, made Wickham marry Lydia. There was no other explanation. It must have cost him a fortune.

She had not even dared to think of asking him for so much. She could not understand why he would go to so much extra trouble, mortification, and expense. Did he want her even deeper in his debt?

In the end, it did not matter why. She decided to allow herself one last night among her family. She would bid them farewell the next day and go to Mr. Darcy.

She did not have the chance to put her plan into action. The next morning her uncle came out of his study accompanied by none other than Mr. Darcy. Elizabeth took an involuntary step back as Mr. Gardiner introduced him to his wife. "And I believe you are already acquainted with my niece, Elizabeth."

Her stomach knotted, wondering what Mr. Darcy had told her uncle about her. She could not have said a word to save her life.

"I have that honour. But I must beg your pardon; I have business elsewhere that cannot wait."

Did he expect her to leave with him? Well, he had done his part, and more. Now it was her turn. She squared her shoulders and offered to see him out. He accepted with a silent bow. Once they were safely out of hearing, she said to him, "When shall I expect to see you again, sir?" She was near enough to see the pulse throbbing in his throat. His scent raised goosebumps on her arms. What would it be like to be engulfed in that smell of spice and new leather?

Something flickered in his eyes, then died, making him

look old beyond his years. "I doubt we will meet again, Miss Bennet. You owe me nothing."

"But…"

He held up his hand to stop her. "Please, no more. You have already told me I am proud, disagreeable, and selfish, and that is enough. I did not think I could sink any further in your esteem, but apparently I was incorrect. You also think me such a rake as to dishonour a gentleman's daughter. If you believe I am the sort of man who would so humiliate any woman, much less one I have loved, by taking advantage of her misfortune, you do not know me at all. I will not inflict myself on you in any way."

His words seemed to hang in the air between them as he gave her a long look, then turned to depart. Elizabeth felt the truth of them like a knife. He was, once again, right. It was like reading his letter once again, discovering the new ways she had misjudged him. Why did she always think the worst of this man? Despite his proud carriage, she had seen the wounded look in his eye. What had she done?

The sound of the front door closing roused her from her thoughts, and she hurried down the hallway and out into the street. He was still there, about to step into his carriage, a deep frown marring his visage. When she touched his arm to gain his attention, he stiffened. "Yes?" he said brusquely.

"You are quite right. I do not know you at all, sir, only my own foolish prejudices. I wish I had known the gentleman you truly are, and not allowed myself to be swayed by misconceptions."

He nodded jerkily, as if her words hurt him.

"I thank you for all you have done. I will never forget it, and I will remember you always in my prayers. It can never be repaid."

His look softened slightly. "I do not deserve such praise. If you wish to repay me, I have only one small request."

"Sir?"

"Though it pained me to see it, I admired your willingness to sacrifice yourself for the sake of your family. It must have taken great strength to offer yourself to a man for whom you had no respect, the last man in the world whose company you desired." He paused to take a deep breath.

"Mr. Darcy, that was based on a mistaken understanding. By that time, your letter had given me to understand that you were indeed a man I could respect, or else I could never have trusted you that far." It was oddly important to her that he understand that.

"But not a man you could trust to do the right thing. My point remains the same. What I would ask is your word that you will never turn to someone else in such an extreme. Should you require assistance, please inform *me*, and no one else."

"You have already done so much, and I have done nothing to deserve it."

His eyes seemed black as the night sky. "Promise me you will tell me if you need help. I do not wish to spend the rest of my life wondering if you are safe."

Her mouth was dry as ashes. "I could not possibly...."

"You owe me this much, Miss Bennet."

She swallowed, her breath tight in her chest. "Very well. You have my word."

He tipped his head with a sardonic air, as if mocking himself. "My thanks, Miss Bennet." With that, he swung himself up into the carriage and closed the door panel.

The coachman clicked his tongue at the horses. As the carriage wheels started to roll, Elizabeth called after him. "God bless you, sir." Then she returned to her room and cried.

If such a thing were possible, Elizabeth's encounter with Mr. Darcy threw her into even lower spirits. The mourning dresses she donned each morning seemed to symbolize more than just the loss of her father. With Lydia's marriage, her own situation was no longer as dire, but she could not help thinking of a certain dark-eyed gentleman and cringing at the remembrance of the things she had said to him through their acquaintance. How heartily she repented every saucy speech, and especially her harsh words! She could hardly bear to think of how far his opinion of her must have fallen. Even her return to Longbourn could not free her mind of him.

Longbourn was not the same, either. Even though she rested her head under its roof each night, she could not feel it was her home. Mr. Collins' frequent pointed reminders that her family's presence was tolerated only at the behest of the nephew of Lady Catherine de Bourgh made certain of that, most especially when he referred to Mr. Darcy as Lady Catherine's future son-in-law. It was almost amusing to realize that Mr. Collins had no idea his demeaning words would strike home so deeply.

But as spring gave way to summer, and then to autumn, Elizabeth's natural spirits began to rise once more. Her future remained uncertain, but she learned once more to take pleasure in the scent of flowers and fresh air on her long rambles through the countryside. It was on her return home from such a walk that she discovered two most unexpected callers in the sitting room with Charlotte and Jane.

At first all she could see was Mr. Darcy. Her feet were rooted to the floor as she felt the heat of mortification rise in her cheeks. It was not until Mr. Bingley spoke that she recognized his presence at Jane's side. She barely managed to stammer out a greeting and to enquire after each of their families.

Both gentlemen responded with warm civility, but Elizabeth's embarrassment was such that she could hardly register their conversation. Why had Mr. Darcy come to Longbourn? Was he simply checking whether Mr. Collins had kept his word to shelter the Bennet family, or could it be that he had another motive? Whenever she dared glance in his direction, she found his gaze firmly fixed on her.

There was no opportunity for private conversation until the gentlemen were leaving. The ladies walked with them outside, Mr. Bingley engaging Jane and Charlotte in lively discussion. The pressure of silence made Elizabeth even more aware of Darcy's scent of fresh leather, and her pulses fluttered in response.

Darcy cleared his throat. "You seemed surprised to see me today."

She gave him a startled glance. "Very much so. I had not known you planned to return to Hertfordshire."

"It was a recent decision." He tugged at his gloves, as if they did not fit properly. "I have thought about what you said, about not knowing me. I came to offer to begin our acquaintance anew, if it is agreeable to you."

It was so unexpected that it took her breath away. The realization that he did not, in fact, think ill of her made an unconscious smile curve her lips. "It would be most agreeable, sir."

His eyes darkened. "It is not unpleasant, then, to see me again?"

Her smile bloomed to cover her face, and she felt that the whole world must smile with her. "I am glad and proud to see you again, Mr. Darcy."

He began to smile as well, and Elizabeth was struck by how handsome it made him appear.

She offered him her hand, and felt an odd shock go through her as he took it in his own. He seemed dumbfounded at first, but then recovered himself to bow over her hand, his eyes never leaving hers. As he pressed his lips against her hand more firmly than propriety would dictate, a novel heat began to move through Elizabeth. If only she could freeze the moment in time! She knew she would relive it again and again in her memory.

Her fingers tingling, she said, "I hope we will meet again soon."

Darcy released her hand with obvious reluctance, then mounted his horse and took the reins in his hand as he looked down at her. "You may depend upon it, Miss Bennet."

He spurred the horse and trotted down the drive. When he turned at the last moment and their eyes met, Elizabeth felt a new warmth deep inside her. Still feeling his kiss on her hand, and walked back into Longbourn with a dreamy smile.

## Part II

IN THE TWO DAYS since Mr. Darcy's arrival in Hertfordshire, Elizabeth thought of little else but him. The exquisite sensation of his lips against her hand and the smoldering look in his dark eyes fought with the older remembrance of offering herself to him - and being refused. She had never wanted him to accept that offer, but still, it was remarkable to think that he might still care for her despite it. She could not understand it, but if care for her he did, she was not about to question her good fortune.

She had hoped the gentlemen might call again that day, though she knew such an event was unlikely, given the speculation that could arise from such pronounced attentions. She was disappointed to find herself to be correct. Her mother had forbidden Jane to leave the house in case Mr. Bingley saw fit to call, and Elizabeth felt obliged to keep her sister company during her imprisonment. The afternoon seemed to last forever, with only the questionable distraction of her mother's constant discourse on the meaning of Mr. Bingley's return.

Finally Elizabeth's restlessness could no longer be contained. She slipped out of the house, through the garden and onto the lane. She paused when she reached the old stone bridge across the river, resting her hands on the side as she gazed down into the slowly moving water. It reflected the earliest of the sunset with mottled gold and red, colours that broke up as the current swirled past the bridge abutments. On a whim, she crossed the bridge and scrambled down the rocky path to the water's edge. She removed one glove and idly leaned down to dip her fingers in the cool water. It slid between her fingertips, and she imagined it running all the way to the sea. With a smile at her own whimsy, she set off down the riverbank path through the tall grass.

She had not gone far before reaching an area of deep mud too wide for her to cross. She considered climbing up the bank to go around it, but decided it was not worth the effort. Instead she perched on a large rock beside the river. She removed her gloves and laid them beside her, then allowed her fingers to trail in the water once again. It was a soothing sensation.

The silence, broken only by occasional birdsong, was interrupted by the sound of hoof beats approaching at a trot, then coming to a halt. Elizabeth glanced toward the bridge and froze. A familiar figure sat on horseback, gazing down into the water just as she had done a few minutes earlier. Elizabeth willed herself invisible, even as she stole the rare opportunity to look her fill on Mr. Darcy, admiring the straightness of his back and his elegant hands casually holding the reins. Then her eyes drifted back to his face, only to discover he was now looking straight at her.

Belatedly he removed his hat and bowed from the saddle, his eyes never leaving her. Elizabeth, blushing, nodded in return, deciding that scrambling to her feet on the uneven ground would hardly appear graceful or ladylike. She felt suddenly burning hot, despite the breeze along the river.

He seemed to hesitate, then crossed the bridge, dismounted and tied his horse to a sapling. Elizabeth's heart beat faster as he made his way carefully down the bank.

Soon he stood before her. "May I have the honour of joining you, Miss Bennet?"

He had never before asked if she desired his company. When they had met on walks in Kent, he had seemed to take it for granted that she would. Elizabeth wondered if the change had been deliberate. Had her criticisms at Hunsford been enough to initiate a alteration of this sort?

"You are quite welcome, sir. There is more than enough river to share." Belatedly she remembered her gloves lying discarded by her side. Without looking at him, she took her hand from the water and dried it with her handkerchief, then slipped on the offending articles. She wondered if he was shocked, and why she cared so much.

"Please do not allow me to interfere with your pleasure in the day," he said formally.

Feeling most uncomfortable, she said, "It is nothing."

"Cool water on a warm day can be refreshing."

What did he want from her? Acknowledgement of her inappropriate behaviour? If that was the case, she would not satisfy him. "Indeed it is. I like to imagine that the water travelling to the sea, and that somehow it would remember my touch as it goes from river to river. Perhaps some day this water will reach lands I have never even imagined."

"Fortunate water." Mr. Darcy set his hat on the stone, then seemed to take a sudden interest in the local flora.

Elizabeth watched from the corner of her eyes as he picked up several twigs, leaves, and odd bits of bark. It seemed somehow out of character for him, but she said nothing as he sat down on the bank and began to combine his finds in different ways, clearly deep in thought. Finally he chose a large leaf and pierced it twice with a twig, then inserted the twig in a piece of bark. He bound the construction with several long strands of grass. Elizabeth smiled as she recognized the rough shape of a boat, with the leaf serving as a sail.

She said archly, "I had not realized you were an expert in maritime construction."

He gave an embarrassed smile. "You should not say that until we see if it is sea-worthy. It has been many years since my cousin and I constructed our own fleets on the lake at Pemberley. The boat that stayed afloat longest was the winner." He examined his creation with a slight frown, then plucked a violet and placed it on the bark. Then he leaned forward and set it on the water in a quiet eddy.

"Did the Pemberley Navy also carry flowers?"

"Never. They were crewed only by our imaginations." He paused. "That was long before either of us recognized the importance of beauty as well as strength."

Elizabeth felt oddly flustered. "Was this cousin Colonel Fitzwilliam?" she said, in an attempt to bring the conversation back to some sort of normalcy.

He glanced at her. "Yes, it was."

She felt her cheeks grow hot. "I hope he is well, and your family at Rosings as well."

"Quite well. I hope the Collinses are well?"

"Indeed so." Suddenly the moment seemed surreal. This was the man she had offered herself to, whom she had expected to share her bed, who knew her darkest secret, and they could do no better at a conversation that stilted formalities. She clapped her hand over her mouth to smother a laugh.

"Something amuses you, Miss Bennet?"

She could not possibly tell him what she had been thinking. "It is nothing, sir, merely a passing thought." She still felt the laughter bubbling up inside of her, and knew it must show in her eyes. She tried to force a solemn look onto her face.

He gave her a long, serious look. "Humour is best when shared."

She shook her head vigourously, biting down hard on her lip to avoid a fit of giggles.

His mouth straightened into a line, and he pulled on his gloves. "I must be on my way," he said flatly, rising to his feet. "I hope you enjoy the day, Miss Bennet."

She was taken aback by his tone, and all desire to laugh disappeared. What had happened to the approachable man who had sought out her company? Why had he turned into the proud stranger she had met at the Meryton Assembly? Then it came clear; he did not know her well enough to be accustomed to her moments of laughter. He had thought her refusal to share her thought was a rejection of him. Could she in truth injure him so easily, without any intention of it?

She did not want him to leave. She scrambled to her feet. "Sir, it was nothing. I did not want to embarrass us both by raising the past, but if you must know, I was thinking how odd it was that, after all we have shared, after all I have done and said, that we had reverted to asking about the health of acquaintances. You must admit it is an odd juxtaposition."

His serious look slowly faded, replaced by a slight smile. "Ours has been an odd acquaintance. I had not anticipated how difficult conversation might be while we are pretending the past never occurred."

She turned her head so she need not meet his eyes, and squinted in the sunlight.

"Miss Bennet?" He sounded uncharacteristically tentative. "I am sorry if my ill-thought words troubled you."

"Not at all, sir, it is only the sun in my eyes. But there is a question I must ask you."

"Yes?" His voice was guarded.

"You know all too well just what I am capable of, what I suggested to you. How can you possibly wish for an acquaintance with such a woman? How can you have any respect for me?" The words came out in a rush.

"I do not think less of you for any of that. I admired, and still admire, your courage and your loyalty to your family. I know you would never have found yourself in such a position but for sheer desperation, and even then, you did not look for assistance for yourself, but for your family. You were ready to sacrifice yourself for their sake. I felt many things that day, but it never occurred to me, then or now, to doubt your intentions. If anyone should feel ashamed of that day, it would be me, not you."

"How can you possibly say that? You were a perfect gentleman, so much so that I thought you might have lost interest in me altogether."

"Miss Bennet, please, let us sit." He held out a hand to her.

She took it tentatively, feeling a shock at his touch, and allowed him to assist her to sit on the rock once again. She felt the heat of his fingers long after he released her hand.

He joined her, then picked up a round stone and began to toy with it. He said in a low voice, "I was tempted. Not to take advantage of you, as it is not in my character, but to use your situation to force you into marrying me. It came down to the same thing, as it was all about my desires and not about your distress. I wanted it badly. There, do you think me such a gentleman now?"

"Even more than I did before. Only a gentleman would master temptation." She did not know what to say, and it seemed that neither did he, for the silence between them grew long.

Finally she said archly, "I am glad, I suppose, to know that I was enough to tempt you."

He half-turned toward her, leaning on one hand, his voice low. "You can have no idea how you tempt me. You tempt me every day with the thought of your laughter, and every night with the thought of touching you. You tempt me with your every smile, your glance, the way you bite your lip when you are concentrating, by the sparkle in your eye when someone challenges you, the way you tilt your head when you are about to tease, by your sweetness when you try to protect someone's feelings. I remember watching you walk past me at Netherfield, and aching to take you into my arms. I remember listening to you play and sing, and thinking you the most fascinating creature I had ever met. I remember how you cared for your sister when she was ill, and how I wished you would care for me in the same way. I remember how your hair glinted in the candlelight at the Netherfield ball, and how I longed to touch it, to take the pins out and watch it tumble around your shoulders. I see the pulse in your neck, and I ache to press my lips to it. I dream of your eyes sparkling for me, your hands reaching for me, your lips against mine. Oh, yes, Elizabeth, you tempt me. Every second, every minute, every hour, every day, waking or sleeping, you tempt me almost beyond reason." His eyes were dark, his voice almost a whisper by the time he finished, but she heard every word of it.

Elizabeth felt suddenly unable to breathe. A new heat flowed through her, and it was as if his lips had indeed branded her neck, his eyes had indeed claimed her for his. She felt aware of her body as she never had before, aching for him to come even closer, yet at the same time fearing it. She could feel the tension radiating from him, and his scent of leather and fresh soap made her dizzy. She was glad she was sitting; had they still been standing, she doubted her legs would have held her. As it was, she felt as if she might melt and run into the river. How could she possibly reply? She touched her tongue to her dry lips.

"Dearest, loveliest Elizabeth," he breathed, his words a caress in themselves, his eyes dropping hungrily to her lips.

She could feel the warmth of his breath on her cheeks. Her heart was pounding so loudly she was sure he must hear it over the gentle murmur of the river. Her world had narrowed to the few inches between them. How could she feel so much heat and still be frozen in place? All her training told her to back away, but every instinct demanded to experience the next step. Admitting the truth to herself, she lifted her chin a fraction of an inch in as much of an invitation as she dared give.

But he did not, as she expected, kiss her. Instead his finger lightly stroked her cheek, then traced the outline of her lips. Somehow that slight touch engendered desires she had never known. Her lips parted on a sigh.

Darcy, sensitized to her every motion, closed his eyes in a half-ecstatic disbelief, focusing all his being on the sense of touch. He did not need to see to find her lips with his; he was drawn to them as if by a magnetic force. The moment seemed to last an eternity until he finally felt the heavenly soft warmth of her lips against his. His tongue traced her lips, and through even that slight touch he could feel her shiver, and his body responded urgently. He had to use his entire force of will to hold back from taking her in his arms, yes, from urging her back so that he could explore every inch of her body and make her his, so she would never leave him again. But if he frightened her off again, he would never forgive himself, and he was already taking a terrible risk of that. Did he imagine her lips moving under his, beginning a tentative response, or was it real? The warmth of her shot through him like lightning. If a mere innocent kiss from Elizabeth drove him to this state of desperation, what would happen when he made love to her? And at that moment, he knew it was within his power, that if he pressed his suit, she would be his. Just as it had been within his power the day she offered herself to him in London.

That memory was enough to jerk him out of the haze of desire that threatened him. He forced himself to pull back. Bereft of even that slight touch, he opened his eyes, only to see the rosiness of her lips and cheeks, her dilated pupils, her soft look that told him she was also in the grip of feelings beyond her control. How could he hold himself back from her implicit invitation?

Elizabeth murmured, "Such a fierce frown, Mr. Darcy. Is that what comes of giving in to temptation?"

Her gentle teasing gave him the distance he needed to regain himself. "No, this is what comes of resisting temptation. If I were any more tempted, I would have to jump into the river to regain my sanity."

She raised an eyebrow. "Your sanity is in the river?"

"I have no sanity where you are concerned."

"I had begun to suspect as much!"

Then, to Darcy's utter astonishment - and bedevilment - Elizabeth clasped her hands behind his neck and swayed toward him, her eyes drifting closed. For a moment he tried to tell himself she did not understand the risk she was taking, but then the long months of agony of wanting her overwhelmed his hesitation. Clasping his arms around her, feeling the exquisite torture of her delicate form pressing against his chest, her scent of lavender and sweet womanhood intoxicating him, he drowned himself in her lips.

Could anything in his life ever be as sweet and dangerous as this moment? He had to taste her skin, of he would die for the need of it. He dusted kisses across her cheek, then nibbled her ear. Her moan in response drove all thought out of his mind. His hands, which he had kept so carefully on her back, began of their own volition an exploration of her curves, stroking down her spine, then, as she made no protest, he brought them nearer and nearer the temptation of her breasts. She apparently wanted the same, for she arched toward him, shattering what little restraint he had remaining. Her breasts fit perfectly into his hands, as if they had been made for this moment. He could not resist running his thumbs over her nipples, eliciting a gasp as he felt them harden beneath his touch.

Then he stopped thinking at all. He claimed her mouth again with a fierce passion, then his lips began a journey downward along the soft, tender skin of his neck, exploring every hollow and tracing his tongue along her collarbone, then down to the tempting flesh below. Her breasts smelled of honeysuckle, and he knew he had to taste them. His fingertip crept below the neckline of her muslin dress, and he was rewarded by another moan, the sweetest sound he had ever heard. Needing no further encouragement, his hand followed his fingertip until he could cup her softness. Ah, a man could die of such sweetness.

Or a man could lose any chance at the future he longed for. "For God's sake, Elizabeth, stop me! Throw me in the river, anything," he pleaded.

Elizabeth had no desire to do so. She had no wish but to have him continue the exquisitely pleasurable torture he was inflicting upon her body, to relieve the aching in her breasts and the tight heat between her legs. But the distress in his voice penetrated her last shred of reason and she pushed him away. For a moment they stared into each other's eyes, each breathing as if they had just run a race, then Elizabeth reached down to adjust her dress. When it was back in place and covering all the revealing flesh, she looked up at Darcy through her lashes with an arch smile. "You overestimate my strength, sir. If you wish to swim, you must do it of your own volition, but I will warn you, the water is very cold indeed."

He shifted away from her and leaned back against his

hands, his face turned upward toward the darkening sky. Elizabeth, though embarrassed beyond measure and uncertain of his mood, could not resist admiring his distinctly carved profile.

She longed to touch his face, to explore it with her fingers and to kiss him once again. No, she longed for far more than that, if she was honest with herself, but this was hardly the time or place, so she carefully folded her hands in her lap and turned her gaze to the setting sun.

After several minutes, he said, "I would feel much better if you did throw me in, or at the very least, slapped my face."

She tilted her head to look at him. "As much as I dislike disappointing you, sir, I fear it is rather too late to slap you. Not to mention that it would be rather hypocritical of me."

He turned tortured eyes to her. "You deserve better than me."

"Because you are tempted by me? It would be a sorry state indeed if you were not. In that case, I might in fact be tempted to slap your face."

"Nonetheless, I apologize for my behaviour."

Oddly, his formality made him seem more like a misbehaving schoolboy, and Elizabeth could not help laughing at the idea. "I hope you do not disapprove of the fact that I enjoyed your behaviour?"

He made a sound deep in his throat. "Miss Bennet, it is time for us to return to civilization. It is growing dark."

"You need not worry. The moonlight will be bright enough to keep us from falling into the river."

"Perhaps so, but I do not trust myself alone with you in the dark." He swallowed hard.

Despite the great pleasure she was taking in teasing him, Elizabeth could tell that she had pushed him far enough. She rose to her feet. "Very well, then, I will take your advice."

She followed Mr. Darcy down the path to the bridge,

setting her feet carefully to avoid tripping. Concentrating on the path provided a distraction from the strange feelings that seemed to have taken over her body, that made her wish he would turn around and kiss her again. The shape of his shoulders in the twilight was enough to make her mouth dry.

Darcy scrambled up the bridge embankment, then reached down to offer her his hand. She felt a shock as she took it. How could a touch of his hand cause her lips to ache to be kissed? With Darcy's assistance, she had little trouble keeping to her feet on the steep slope. At the top, however, she found herself standing bare inches from him, their hands still clasped. His face was in shadow, but she could feel the intensity of his attention.

When he spoke, his voice was half-strangled. "I will speak with your cousin in the morning."

"No! Please do not. I am of age. I do not need his permission, and his loyalty to Lady Catherine is such that he might refuse it in any case."

At least she had not refused his implicit proposal. "May I call on you, then?" It would seem like a lifetime till tomorrow morning, but there was nothing to be done for it.

"My mother is expecting callers in the morning, and you would not enjoy the experience. Perhaps we could meet here in the afternoon?"

"I will be here." He was clearly still struggling with himself.

Then his control broke. She found his arms around her, her body pressed against the hardness and strength of his, her head tilted back to receive a kiss that was as different from his earlier ones as a tempest from a spring rain shower. His lips were pressed hard against hers, as if he were striving to make them one body. His tongue teased her lips apart, opening her to the astonishing intimacy as he explored her mouth possessively. She did not want him to ever stop.

But he did, pulling away and then running both hands through his hair. After a moment, he said, "May I walk with you back to Longbourn?"

She smiled at him, her heart still fluttering. "I would be very happy if you did."

They did not speak much as they walked, Elizabeth allowing herself to be far closer to him that propriety would dictate, and his free hand covering hers tenderly where it lay on his arm. She had never realized how intimate the act of taking a gentleman's arm could be. If she became any more attuned to his every breath and movement, she would go up in flames.

He bade her a very proper adieu when they reached the house. She watched as he walked away, then entered Longbourn. It felt like she was a different person than she had been when she had left it a few hours earlier. Something had been awakened in her, something that would never rest. She wished only to be alone to think back on what had happened. She spent but a few minutes with her family before retiring early. To her relief, Mr. Collins seemed unusually abstracted and did not hold forth at length as he had so often since taking possession of Longbourn.

Elizabeth was roused from a deep sleep by Hill shaking her shoulder and whispering, "Wake up, Miss Elizabeth. We must get you dressed and ready to go."

"Go where?" Elizabeth asked, rubbing her eyes.

"Shh!" the housekeeper said, gesturing to Jane's sleeping body. "Mr. Collins says your aunt Gardiner is terrible sick, like to die, and your uncle begs you to come to London immediately."

"My aunt?" Pain struck in the pit of her stomach. It could not be. Mrs. Gardiner was rarely ill. "I must go. When is the first post?"

"Mr. Collins will take you himself. He says there is no time to waste. He is having the carriage drawn up now."

Elizabeth struggled into her dress as Hill quickly packed a small bag for her. She was still blinking sleep out of her eyes as she went downstairs to find Mr. Collins waiting impatiently at the door.

"Come, Cousin Elizabeth. There is not a moment to lose." He hurried her out the door.

The lanterns were lit on the carriage. Fortunately, the moon was bright enough that they should be able to make respectable time even at night. But that reminded her of Mr. Darcy and she stopped short. What would he think when she did not arrive at their assignation? Surely he would understand when he discovered the circumstances.

Mr. Collins handed her into the carriage, then took the seat opposite and rapped on the roof for the driver to start. Elizabeth did not want to talk to him, so she huddled under the carriage rug and closed her eyes. Despite her intense worry, the rocking of the carriage lulled her into a dozing state.

When she awoke, it was full light outside. They must be near London by now. She opened the window shade to check, and saw a rolling landscape with a line of hills just beyond. She blinked at it in confusion, but it remained the same. She turned to Mr. Collins in agitation. "Did we take the wrong fork? This is not the road to London!"

Mr. Collins smirked, seemingly untroubled by this intelligence. "No, my dear cousin, it is not."

## Part III

Simms halted in the doorway of the study and bowed fastidiously. Without looking up, Darcy said, "I am not at home." He was in no mood for callers. As far as he was concerned, he might never be in the mood for them again.

The butler paused a minute longer than he usually would, then said, "I will tell Miss Bennet. Shall I indicate that you are unlikely to be at home to her in the future?"

Darcy's hand jerked, knocking over the inkwell and spreading a pool of black ink over the letter he had just finished. He glared at Simms as if suggesting it was his fault. "Miss Bennet is not in London," he said coldly, carelessly tossing a fresh sheet of paper over the large blot. He did not know what sort of joke this was, but it was not in the least amusing.

"Miss Bennet is on the doorstep, sir. She was quite insistent that I see if you were at home."

Darcy knew Simms would never joke. Then he realized what the butler had said. "You left her on the doorstep? Show her in at once."

Simms looked taken aback by his unexpected harshness. "To the sitting room, sir?"

Darcy scowled. With ink all over his desk, he could not receive Elizabeth in the study where he would be able to sit with the safety of his desk between them. "The sitting room, yes."

"Right away, sir." Simms hurried away.

As Darcy stood and hurriedly straightened his waistcoat, he noticed an ink stain on his right sleeve. Of all the times to turn accident-prone!

He must calm himself. There was no telling what had brought Elizabeth here, and he would not raise his hopes again only to have them cruelly extinguished. But he would not keep her waiting.

As he strode down the hallway, he heard her familiar light tones thanking Simms, no doubt for taking her bonnet and pelisse. His gut wrenched at the sound. He hastened into the sitting room, choosing to stand behind a sofa tall enough to hide the stain on his sleeve. He closed his eyes, taking a deep breath to calm himself.

"Mr. Darcy?" Elizabeth's amusement at catching him unawares as she entered was clear.

His eyes shot open. What was wrong with Simms today, first leaving a lady on the doorstep and then failing to announce her presence? "Miss Bennet." He bowed stiffly and gestured to a chair, careful to use his left arm.

He waited for her to begin, but she seemed at a loss as well. Finally they both spoke at the same moment, and both stopped with apologies to the other. Darcy said, "Pray, continue."

Elizabeth folded her hands in her lap and looked down at them for a moment, then straightened her back and looked him in the eye. "Some time ago, you elicited from me a promise that if I found myself in desperate circumstances again, I would inform you. I seem to be making a habit of desperation."

Had her lover abandoned her? Did she truly expect him to help her now? It did not matter; he knew he would help her no matter the circumstances. He had no choice. "What difficulties are you facing?" His voice sounded unnecessarily harsh to his ear.

She raised a playful eyebrow, though her eyes did not sparkle as they did when she was truly amused. "Quite similar to the last time, in fact. Mr. Collins has given me two options. One is to continue to live at his sister's home in Dorset as a virtual prisoner. If I agree to that, my family may remain at Longbourn. If I return to Meryton, or if I seek out my other relations, he will put my mother and sisters out on the street. I am constitutionally not suited to imprisonment, so I have left his sister's home. I have a small amount of money that I brought from home, enough to cover today's post to London, and while it should be sufficient to purchase a few nights' shelter, it will not go far. I hope you find that suitably desperate?"

It made no sense. "A virtual prisoner? Surely you overstate the matter."

She shrugged lightly, her face unusually still. "It seemed so to me. I was locked in my room for over a fortnight, and the door was only opened for meals and other necessities. To be fair, Mr. Collins had told his sister that I could have the freedom of the house as soon as I gave my word not to leave nor to make any effort to contact anyone, but as you can see, I was not willing to make that promise."

"If you were locked in your room, how then are you here?"

Her face paled. "When it became clear that I was to be left to my own resources, I climbed out the window. It was not difficult, I had merely hoped to be spared the indignity of running away." She rose to her feet. "I see now that was a foolish hope. I will bid you good day, sir. I am sorry to have troubled you." Her voice trembled as she turned away.

Was she trying to play him for a fool? "What happened to the officer?"

She turned slightly over her shoulder, blinking rapidly. "What officer?"

"The officer with whom you eloped. Did he abandon you so quickly?" He had not meant to say that, but his bitterness would not be restrained.

Her eyes widened. "Is that what they told you?"

"It was general knowledge."

Elizabeth made a hissing sound between her teeth. "It must be Mr. Collins' doing. I assure you, I did not leave Longbourn with anyone besides him and the driver of the carriage. I thought I was travelling to help my aunt Gardiner, who was said to be near death, and by the time that I noticed in my distress that we were not on the road to London, we were hours from Longbourn in unknown country. I had no choice but to proceed."

Darcy's mouth was suddenly dry. Could it possibly be true? "Why would Mr. Collins have done such a thing?"

Elizabeth crossed her arms as if to protect herself. "Surely you can guess that."

"I cannot."

She sighed. "He believed I had entered into an improper liaison with you. He thought to spare his own reputation, and I do not doubt that he hoped for some sort of reward from Lady Catherine de Bourgh as well. Had he known that you had already rejected my *favours* once, perhaps he would have been less disquieted." The burning irony in her voice was unmistakable. "Then again, I would have thought you would not have believed such a story about me, but, as we both have cause to know, I have a history of being incorrect in my judgments regarding you. But I will trouble you no further. Good day, Mr. Darcy."

She was already at the door before he shook off the paralysis that held him captive. He reached her in a few quick strides and gripped her arm, turning her to face him. "Elizabeth, I did not know. I swear it to you. I would have hunted for you the entire length of England had I known."

"Yet you believed that I would accept your kisses one day, and run off with another man the next? Of course, I should not blame you, since you already know the depths to which I can sink." Her words hung in the air like a knife.

"I was a fool. A broken-hearted fool. But even your sister did not deny what had happened. Who was I to question her word?" As he said it, he recalled the frightened look on Jane Bennet's face, and her frequent glances at Mr. Collins, when he finally called at Longbourn to ask after Elizabeth. Why had he not suspected a deception?

Elizabeth gave him a silent grave look, then carefully removed his hand from her arm and turned once more to go.

Surely he could not lose her again? "Elizabeth, please do not leave."

She ignored him.

"You have no place to go," he said in desperation, following her into the hallway.

"You need not worry. I am not completely without resources."

Was he going to have to chase her into the street? "Miss Bennet," he said firmly, in his best Master of Pemberley voice.

She stopped, but did not turn back to him. He could tell she was wavering, but her pride was injured.

"Miss Bennet, some time ago, as you say, you offered yourself to me under terms of my choice, provided that I assisted your family. I kept my part of the bargain, and now I am ready to state my terms."

Her back stiffened abruptly. After a moment of silence, she said in the most even of tones, "And what are your terms?"

Relief began to trickle through him. "My terms are that you shall remain under this roof."

She turned slowly, her eyes wide. "That would destroy anything that remains of my reputation."

"Perhaps," he said more gently, and began to let his smile show through. "But my sister can serve as your chaperone, and since you will be accompanying me to Doctors' Common early tomorrow morning to obtain a special license and we will be wed by noon, it will be of little matter."

He could almost see her relief as the sparkle returned to her fine eyes. She smiled archly and said, "It is dangerous to assume a lady's consent to a proposal of marriage."

Now his smile could not be repressed. "As I have cause to

know. But in this case, I need not concern myself with such small details, since I am entitled to state the terms."

She crossed her arms in front of her and attempted to look stern, but he could see her eyes were laughing. "Just how long do you intend to hold me to this bargain? Am I to be your servant all my life?"

He could no longer stay away. He took her hands, pressing the lightest of kisses first into one palm, and then the other. "I will consider your debt paid in full as soon as you have vowed before God to love, honour and obey me." Her nearness made him dizzy with longing.

"I see that you are indeed a man who likes to have his own way!" she said.

He was beyond relieved that she was teasing him again. "Please believe me, Elizabeth, if I had known you left Longbourn against your wishes, I would not have left a stone unturned in all England until I found you. I should have known not to believe the lies I was told, but it does not reflect on my respect for you and your word, but only upon my own uncertainty that you could ever regard me with affection after all that has happened in the past."

She tilted her head to one side. "Then tell me, what must I do to convince you of my regard?"

He took her hands in his and held them tightly. "Tell me that you will marry me tomorrow."

"Since I have nowhere else to go, it would seem wise."

"Elizabeth, do not tease me now. I am at your mercy."

"Very well, then, I will marry you tomorrow." She raised one hand to touch him lightly on the cheek.

His breath caught in his throat. He whispered, "May I kiss you?"

She smiled. "You are the one stating the terms."

He stepped closer, until there was barely an inch between

their bodies. "You know I could never do anything to you that was truly against your will. You are my dearest, loveliest Elizabeth, and I will devote my life to making you as happy as you have made me at this moment."

Her eyes gazed deeply into his with a joy he had never seen in them before. "Then perhaps you might begin by kissing me, but it might be best if you remove your coat first. It would look highly improper if my dress had ink stains to match your coat sleeve."

He did not need a second invitation. He stripped off his topcoat and threw it across the back of the sofa, heedless of the upholstery.

Elizabeth, with an impish look, folded back the sleeve of his coat. "We cannot have you staining the upholstery, either."

"If it is stained, I will throw it away and buy a new one. I would buy an entire houseful of new furniture if it meant I could kiss you."

His arms were warm around her, and there was something more intimate now that he was in his shirtsleeves. It was an embrace of the sort she had only pictured between husband and wife, and the notion sent a deep thrill through her. Tomorrow she would be his wife in truth and discover all the mysteries of the marriage bed. The ache deep within her intensified as she felt his kiss lightly brushing her cheek, then trailing a line of fire along her jaw until finally reaching her burning lips. A moan escaped her as his tongue teased her into deepening the kiss, plunging her into that sweet intimacy that had haunted her dreams since their encounter on the riverbank. Their tongues danced together, and she could feel his passion as he crushed her against him.

The fire was now running through every inch of her. Her breasts ached for his touch, and the rough cloth of her shift rubbing against her was not an adequate substitute. She needed more, oh, so much more. But as the sweet oblivion of desire washed over her, the sound of footsteps in the hall made them jump apart. Elizabeth could think of nothing beyond the urge to be back in his arms, and she knew she must look even more disheveled than when she had arrived. Fortunately, Darcy stepped in front of her just as two maids appeared in the doorway, each carrying a tray.

"Mr. Simms said you would want refreshments, sir," the older one said.

"Refreshments?" Darcy looked as if he had never heard of such a concept before. "Ah, yes. Please set them up."

It seemed to take forever for the maids to arrange the dishes on the side table. Elizabeth wondered if they guessed what their master had been doing, and if so, what they would think of her.

But once they had left, and Elizabeth found herself engulfed in his embrace, nothing else mattered. She leaned against his shoulder. She had never realized that a man's arms could provide such comfort and solace, not to mention the myriad other sensations she felt. Then, to her surprise, he released her, keeping only her hand in his.

His eyes were dark with desire. "I can be trusted no further. Pardon me a moment." Reluctantly he dropped her hand, then exited the room without a further word.

Darcy tried to still his breathing. He was not surprised to find Simms hovering in the drawing room. "Simms, Miss Bennet will be staying the night. I believe the blue room would suit admirably."

Simms' eyes widened. "The blue room, sir?"

"That is what I said."

The butler bowed rigidly. "It will be prepared immediately."

"One more thing, Simms. Miss Bennet should be treated with all the respect due to the future Mrs. Darcy." It felt remarkably good to say.

The normally poker-faced Simms broke into a stunned smile. "Congratulations, sir."

"I thank you."

Darcy leaned a hand against the wall. He needed to think, something that was remarkably difficult when his entire being was demanding that he return to Elizabeth and lock the sitting room door behind him. Despite the overwhelming temptation, he would not dishonour her so. He stopped a footman and told him that Miss Darcy's presence was requested in the sitting room. That would provide some restraint. He returned to the sitting room, forcing himself to leave the door wide open.

Elizabeth was loading a small plate with fruits and pastries. She gave him a half-guilty glance. "I hope you will forgive me that I did not wait for you. I have eaten nothing today, and I did not wish to celebrate our reunion by swooning with hunger."

His eyes widened with horror. "Elizabeth! You should have said something immediately. Here, you must sit down and eat. I will bring you anything you like. Shall I ring for some cold meats? A glass of wine?" He placed a hand under her elbow and led her to the sofa as if she might have somehow have forgotten how to get there. How could he have been thinking only of his desire for her and not of her comfort?

"This will do quite nicely." Elizabeth took a bite of cherry pastry as he sat beside her protectively, far closer than propriety would dictate. "It is delicious."

Another surge of desire went through him as her tongue captured a crumb that remained on her upper lip. He chastised himself silently, noticing for the first time her pallor and that her hand trembled slightly as she set her fork into a strawberry. He would never allow her to suffer so again, not now that she was under his protection.

Darcy felt he had come off fairly well, all things considered. Georgiana seemed pleased to be introduced to Elizabeth, at least after she recovered from the shock of finding him in his shirtsleeves with an arm around an unknown young lady. He had expected the news of their wedding the following day to provoke even greater surprise and perhaps some embarrassing questions, but instead Georgiana seemed nothing more than delighted to have a new sister so very quickly.

His housekeeper managed to find a dress of Georgiana's that fit Elizabeth presentably, and Georgiana's maid had restored Elizabeth's appearance to something more closely resembling its usual state. Not that Darcy cared for himself; he found Elizabeth beautiful no matter her circumstances, and her earlier dishevelment had only made her seem even more desirable.

He managed to keep his hands to himself for the remainder of the day, or at least mostly so. He had not been able to resist the exquisite temptation of taking Elizabeth's hand while Georgiana played the pianoforte for them after dinner, tracing circles in her palm with his fingers as her cheeks grew becomingly flushed and he grew ever more aroused.

If it were not for his sister's presence, it would have been a difficult, if not impossible, feat to resist kissing Elizabeth at every available opportunity. The swift shift from his earlier hopelessness to his present happiness was intoxicating. He refused to think about the wedding night tomorrow, lest his remaining self-possession be endangered.

In his efforts to avoid thinking of Elizabeth and bedrooms, however, he had neglected to plan ahead to the moment when they would retire for the night. Georgiana seemed to be the first to recognize the awkwardness, but as the hostess, she could not retire first. It would be rude for Darcy to allow Elizabeth to walk to her room alone, especially as it was by his own.

Elizabeth allowed Darcy to lead her through a private sitting room to a large bedroom decorated in shades of blue. A maid stood in the corner, clearly awaiting her. She explored the room briefly, hardly able to believe that she would be staying in such elegance. Running her finger along the intricately carved edge of the vanity, she smiled at Darcy.

"I hope you will be comfortable here," he said, standing stiffly just outside the door.

"How could I be anything else? It is truly lovely."

"Blue was my mother's favorite colour, but of course you may prefer to redecorate it." He seemed somehow larger in this setting.

Elizabeth started. She had assumed it was a guest room. Her mouth grew dry at the thought that tomorrow night he would be coming to her there, and her breasts ached for his touch. Her instinct was to run into his arms, but she knew she could not obey it. "It reminds me of the sky on a summer's day." Or perhaps it was the heat burning inside her that made her think of summer. How was she to say goodnight to him?

"My room is on the other side." He pointed to another door off the sitting room. "If you find yourself in need of anything, just ring and one of the servants will come."

She walked closer to him and took his hand. "You are very kind."

He drew her aside a step, out of the view of the maid. "Elizabeth, once your maid leaves, I want you to lock the door."

She touched his lips with one finger that trembled slightly. "I have no concerns."

He drew in a sharp breath. "Have I not told you that you tempt me quite beyond reason? There is only so much a man can bear, no matter how good his intentions."

She stood on tiptoe and brushed her lips against his lingeringly. "I will bid you good night, then."

"Damn the servants," he muttered. He pulled her into his arms, kissing her with such thoroughness that Elizabeth felt her knees grow weak. His tongue danced with hers, sending a shock of desire straight to her most secret places. The kiss lasted only a minute, though it could have been an hour and it would still not have been long enough.

Darcy, breathing heavily, took several steps back. If he did not let her go this instant, he would drag her into his bedroom and make her his in every way. The image of Elizabeth in his bed, every inch of her displayed for his view, her face drugged with desire, her hair spread across the pillow was almost his undoing. He clenched his hands into fists and made a proper bow to her.

He could hardly bear it as the door closed behind her. Such a permeable barrier, just a door, but it must stand. He should be grateful that Elizabeth was here and would be his tomorrow. His loins ached painfully with need.

He gritted his teeth as he turned to his room. He allowed his valet to assist him in removing his frock coat and boots, but then dismissed him. His condition was all too apparent in his tight breeches without exposing himself further. He threw himself into his favorite chair and stared into the fire, trying to force himself to think of anything but Elizabeth only a room away, in the room that he had always dreamed would be hers.

Then he laughed suddenly. His sufferings now, such as they were, were nothing to what he had felt only a few hours earlier, believing that Elizabeth had run off with another man, and he would never see her again. To have had his hopes raised in Hertfordshire, only to have them demolished, leaving him worse off than before. Now Elizabeth was his, and she would be his wife in a matter of hours. Elizabeth, his sweetest, loveliest Elizabeth. And all he needed to do was to make it through a night of frustrated desire!

He had to admit it was *very* frustrated desire. Having had

his dreams of Elizabeth snatched away so many times before, part of him could not believe that it would not happen again. But he would not let himself think that way. Instead, he remembered how she had kissed him.

He poured himself a generous glass of brandy and took up the book he had been reading, but then he set it down unread. He could not have taken in a word it said. Instead, he leaned back and sipped his brandy, staring into the fire and thinking of Elizabeth.

He must have drifted off to sleep. He was having the most marvelous dream. Elizabeth, clad in nothing more than a nightgown that did nothing to disguise her form, her curls tumbling in loose glory over her shoulders, leaned over him, her hand on his wrist. He breathed deeply of her fragrance of lavender and womanhood as it drifted past him. Odd, he did not recall dreaming of scents in the past.

Suddenly he was awake. It was no dream. It was the real Elizabeth, more lovely and desirable than ever. Automatically he averted his eyes from her, then a moment later they swerved back. If heaven was going to send him an opportunity to enjoy the sight Elizabeth in a flimsy shift, he was going to appreciate every second of it.

"Is anything amiss?" he managed to say.

"Only that I missed you, and you fell asleep in your chair. And *you* did not lock *your* door."

"You should not be here."

"So everyone would say. But this last fortnight has been dreadful for me, not knowing what had happened to you or why you had not come after me, and wondering if you had a change of heart. Now that I am finally here, I find I cannot bear to be parted from you."

One fact managed to penetrate his sleep-fogged mind:

Elizabeth needed comforting. As if it were the most natural thing in the world to do, he drew her onto his lap and held her soft, yielding form against him. When she laid her head on his shoulder, he thought life could never be sweeter than it was at that moment. "I was missing you as well," he confessed.

"Do you know, while I was locked in that room for two weeks with nothing but a Bible to read, I spent hours just dreaming of being with you?"

"I cannot say I am sorry to hear it. You cannot know how often I have sat in the room which is now yours, grieving that you would never be there in your rightful place."

"My rightful place?" she teased. "You are a gentleman of firm opinions, I see."

"For myself, not for you. You have always been free to make your own decisions, but since I met you, I have never been able to picture another woman as my love. You were always here with me, in my heart."

"You shall hear no complaint from me on that regard, sir." Elizabeth laid her open hand against his chest.

"You need not call me sir, Elizabeth," he said tenderly.

"Shall I call you Fitzwilliam, then?"

"I would like that." In fact, he liked it so much that he could not resist lifting her chin and kissing her, first brushing her lips with his, then, finding himself needing more, deepening the kiss, his tongue meeting hers in an ancient dance that set a fire deep in his groin. Her response was everything he could wish for, all the passion he had always sensed in Elizabeth coming to life as she tangled her fingers in his hair. He relished the sweet taste of her and the warm softness of her lips. He told himself it would just be for one more minute, and then he would stop. Just one more minute. Just one more.

Then he felt Elizabeth's hand lightly probing his chest, her fingertips tantalizingly touching the bare skin beneath his neck revealed by his open shirt. Good God, how much more could he desire her? He strained to hold her closer, which was a better option than allowing his own hands to explore her body, because if he started to do that, he might never be able to stop. But when her fingertip strayed beneath the collar of his shirt, he was overwhelmed by a surge of desire that made him press himself up against her in desperate longing. Just one more minute!

Somehow he found the strength to tear his mouth from hers. His breathing ragged, he said, "Elizabeth, I am only human. We must stop this."

She nibbled his earlobe. "Why?"

How could he possibly think while she was arousing every inch of his body? "Because we are not married yet."

"And that, my love, is precisely why we should not stop." Her lips moved along the sensitive skin of his neck, making him groan. Good God, had she somehow had lesson in how to torture a man, or was it simply natural talent?

The hot blood rushing through his body made it impossible to understand her. Or perhaps it was merely his wishful thinking that she might be telling him not to stop, but that could not be. "Not stop?" he managed to say.

She pulled away just far enough that she could look into his eyes. "Once I offered myself to you in exchange for your assistance. Tomorrow night I will be your wife, and it will be my duty to accept your attentions. Tonight is the only moment when I can come freely to you for no reason but that I love you, trust you, and wish to be with you. And that is why I am here."

"Elizabeth," he said, deeply moved. "You honour me. But it is my hope that duty will never be the reason you give yourself to me."

A corner of her mouth quirked up. "Not *solely* duty, or even primarily, of course. It is just the knowledge that the duty exists that makes it less of a free choice. After all we have been through, I want you to have no doubt that I am coming to you freely." With those words, she arched herself against him and wound her arms around his neck.

The softness of her breasts pressed against him drove any rational thought from his mind. His hand, travelling to cup her tender flesh, made the astonishing discovery that she was wearing nothing at all beneath her shift. He might have still managed to assert control over himself, but at that point Elizabeth moaned involuntarily, her eyes drifting closed with pleasure at his touch.

Suddenly he could not recall why there was any decision to be made. Nothing could be more right or more natural than for him to love and pleasure the woman in his arms, to make her his in every way, to make certain that nothing short of death could ever part them again. "Ah, Elizabeth, my dearest, loveliest Elizabeth," he murmured. In one swift movement, he stood, with his tempting burden in his arms.

Elizabeth felt herself being gently placed on his bed, barely aware of anything beyond Darcy's passion-darkened eyes and the astonishing sensations rushing through her. Her body ached for his, but instead of joining her, he stood over her and trailed his finger down the side of her face, then her neck, seeming to leave a fiery path in its wake. When he reached the sensitive notch at the base of her throat, she strained upward in a desire for more.

Darcy's smile was incandescent as he sat down beside her, his hands moving the untie the ribbons of her nightgown. Elizabeth gasped as his lips skimmed along behind his hands, pushing away the fine lawn until her upper half was exposed. She moaned as his hands cupped her breasts, anxious for more of the pleasure he had given her on the riverbank, but it was his mouth, not his fingers, that found her most sensitive spots, sucking and teasing with his tongue until a sharp craving plunged through her, seeming to lead straight to her womb and between her legs. Then his hand was rucking up the bottom of her nightgown, over her ankles and past her knees till she felt the cool air touching the heat of her thighs. His mouth still in possession of her breast, Darcy's hand reached into her most secret places with a tantalizing touch that only made her crave more. She twined her hands in his hair again, holding him tightly to her as if he were her only hope. When he finally began to explore her wetness, she writhed in an agony of need for something she could not even define. Her need threatened to consume her as intense jolts of pleasure rocked through her, building and building until at last she exploded into a fountain of ecstasy, her body shuddering uncontrollably.

As she finally returned to herself, an astonishing lassitude consuming her, she found him looking into her eyes, his fingers still touching her intimately.

"Ah, my Elizabeth," he whispered. "My dearest, loveliest Elizabeth." He straightened and stripped off his shirt.

Elizabeth was so mesmerized by the sight of his muscled torso that she did not even realize that his breeches had followed his shirt until he moved to cover her with his body, pressing hard against the part of her that was still throbbing from his earlier ministrations. Instinctively she parted her legs to make room for him, even as the astonishingly intimate sensation of his hot skin pressed against her breasts made her gasp.

Then she felt her secret places stretching, making room as his hardness pressed into her, claiming her in the most primal of ways. She could tell when he reached resistance, and braced herself for the pain she knew was to come. But he distracted her by kissing her tantalizingly and murmuring words of love, so that he was able to plunge into her, and the sharp pain was over almost before it was begun. She felt herself filled as she never had been before, and knew that she was now bound forever to him.

He began to move within her moistness, very slowly at first, and then in a rhythm that seemed as natural to her as her heartbeat. To her astonishment, the sense of need returned more strongly than she had known it before, coiling and twisting inside her until it reached a near-unbearable urgency. She clasped her legs around him, pulling him even deeper into her, seeking to become one with him. Then he threw back his head, a guttural cry of triumph emerging from his throat, as he once again plunged into her, and this time she convulsed around him as she succumbed completely to pleasure.

Darcy shifted his weight until he lay beside her, his legs still tangled with hers. He rested his head against the silkiness of her hair as it spread along the pillow, just as he had so often dreamed. He held her close, treasuring every moment, wondering if life could ever be better than it was now. He did not want to ever let Elizabeth out of his arms.

Eventually she stirred, and said, "I must return to my room soon."

"Must you?" he said with a slight smile. He was already beginning to desire her again.

"Yes, I must," she said archly. "I do not wish to be found here in the morning, and I must sleep. In case you have not heard, I am to be married tomorrow and will need my rest."

He laughed low in his throat. "I suppose I cannot argue with that reasoning." Especially as he suspected she had not slept much the previous night, if at all. A wave of tenderness swept over him. Taking care of her must come first. She had already given him her most precious gift, and he must not be greedy.

He did not argue as she tied the ribbons of her nightgown, just kissed her tenderly as she prepared to leave. When her hand was on the doorknob he said, "Elizabeth?"

She gave him a luminous smile. "Yes?"

He came to stand beside her and twined a lock of her hair around his fingers. "You must allow me to tell you how ardently I admire and love you. And you must allow me to tell you that frequently."

She put her arms around him in a brief embrace. "If you continue in that vein, I may not be able to leave!"

"You have discovered my plan," he teased. "Sleep well, my precious Elizabeth." He watched as she glided across the sitting room and into her room. His own room seemed remarkably empty.

Elizabeth woke to a hand on her shoulder, uncertain at first where she was. The room was completely dark except for the glowing embers in the fireplace. Then she recognized the presence beside her, and remembered the many events of the day - and the night. "Fitzwilliam?"

He laid his hand on her cheek. "I thought I warned you to lock your door," he said lightly.

She gave a wicked smile. "*I* thought it would no longer be necessary."

His hand began to move, caressing first her face, then her neck, then travelling down to capture her breast in his hand. "It is now *my* turn to say that I found I could not bear to be parted from you, even for these few hours. Just as you came to me, now I am coming to you."

With her body already beginning to long for his, Elizabeth could barely remember why she had returned to her bedroom in the first place. This was how it should be, and how it should always have been between the two of them. She held her arms out to him as if it were the most natural thing in the world - as perhaps it was - and he came into them with warm sense of belonging and deepest love.

# A Succession of Rain

*Years ago, Amber Lore, the founder of the now-defunct Austen website Hyacinth Gardens, issued a challenge to me. We'd both write stories with dramatic tension without angst, stories where there was no antagonist, no misfortunes or misunderstandings, no interfering relations or embarrassing scenes. Amber, of course, had something written within weeks, while it took years for this story to percolate out of me. Nothing bad happens to the main characters except that it's raining outside. Fortunately, Elizabeth and Darcy are quite able to provide their own dramatic tension!*

"I AM NOT INDEBTED FOR MY PRESENT HAPPINESS TO YOUR EAGER DESIRE OF EXPRESSING YOUR GRATITUDE. I WAS NOT IN A HUMOUR TO WAIT FOR ANY OPENING OF YOUR'S. MY AUNT'S INTELLIGENCE HAD GIVEN ME HOPE, AND I WAS DETERMINED AT ONCE TO KNOW EVERY THING."

- JANE AUSTEN, *PRIDE & PREJUDICE*

ELIZABETH COULD NOT HELP but wonder whether Mr. Darcy would ever return to Meryton, or whether his aunt's particular brand of persuasion had found its mark and convinced him of the ills of marriage so far below his station. She half-expected that Mr. Bingley would receive a letter of excuse from his friend, but instead he was able to bring Darcy with him to Longbourn before many days had passed after Lady Catherine's visit. The gentlemen arrived early, despite the rain that drenched the roads. Elizabeth was proud of herself for the composure with which she met them. She smiled at Mr. Bingley before she turned to his friend, as would be expected from the slight acquaintance she was supposed to have with Mr. Darcy.

She saw immediately that his eyes were on her, though his countenance was serious. A slow warmth and an inexplicable shyness filled her at the notion of what his aunt might have told him, if she had carried out her threat to speak with him.

Mrs. Bennet greeted them both, but without her usual coolness for Mr. Darcy. Elizabeth sat in dread of the reason. Her mother could never keep gossip to herself, nor could she be silent about anything which might add to the importance of her family. Elizabeth briefly considered excusing herself, but that might only draw attention to the situation.

Mrs. Bennet said, "Mr. Darcy, I hope your business in London was successfully concluded."

He bowed in acknowledgment. "Indeed it was, but I am glad to have returned again. London, unlike Hertfordshire, bears no great attraction at this time of year."

Elizabeth risked a glance at him, wondering if this could possibly be meant as a compliment to herself. She met his gaze immediately, raising her suspicions and hopes that it might be the case. Embarrassed, she looked away quickly. It would not do for any of her family to notice a connection between them.

"You cannot imagine who called on us last week, Mr. Darcy," Mrs. Bennet announced with a certain pride.

"I am sure I cannot, but I hope you will enlighten me."

"Why, none other than your aunt, Lady Catherine de Bourgh!" she announced triumphantly. "It was most civil of her, given that her acquaintance with Lizzy was really very trifling, but she was kind enough to give us news of the Collins'."

Elizabeth had rarely wished so hard for the power to become invisible. Her cheeks burned. If Mr. Darcy asked any questions about his aunt's visit, she was sure she might die of humiliation.

"So I have heard, Mrs. Bennet. My aunt called on me lately in London as well, and mentioned the occasion of meeting you."

That was it. She *was* going to die of humiliation.

Her mother then turned the conversation to her favourite topic, Jane's nuptials. Elizabeth could hardly bear to listen, although she noticed Mr. Darcy remained civil in his replies, even when Mrs. Bennet was at her silliest. She dared not look up again, and he did not address her directly. She could not imagine what he must be thinking of her.

It was a question she asked herself again many times during the next week. Darcy called at Longbourn each day despite the inclement weather. Kitty grew fretful as the days went on without even the variety of a trip to Meryton, and Mary had taken it upon herself to offer even more moral platitudes than usual. Mrs. Bennet talked endlessly of the wedding, and Elizabeth felt each day more humiliated by her family. There was never an opportunity to speak with Darcy alone, and if he held her in any particular regard, the only sign of it was his increased civility to her family. She almost wished he would not call at all.

Darcy had several choices, as he saw it. He could call at Longbourn and drag Elizabeth bodily away from her family to some room where they could speak privately. He could take an impossible risk and ask Mr. Bennet for permission to court Elizabeth. Or he could wait for the rain to stop, and hope to get her out of doors where he might have a chance to say his piece. The difficulty with the first two options was that Elizabeth would likely never forgive him. The problem with waiting for the weather to change was that it might drive him out of his mind.

Seven days of rain! Light rain, heavy rain, thunderstorms. Cold, nasty rain. Did the sun never shine in Hertfordshire? Or were the fates simply conspiring against him, as they had in Lambton, causing Elizabeth to leave just as he hoped they might come to an understanding? He paced the floor again.

Why was her behaviour so changed from what it had been at Pemberley? There she had smiled readily, conversed, exchanged glances, but now her eyes were downcast as often as not. Instead of having the pleasure of seeing the sparkling intelligence in her fine eyes, he was reduced to watching the blushes on her cheek and wondering what they might portend. Were they a sign of pleasant awareness of him, or the embarrassment of dealing with an unwanted suitor who kept coming back, despite her best efforts to discourage him? The question kept him from sleep and haunted his days.

Perhaps he *should* speak to Mr. Bennet. At least then he would have an answer one way or another, and if it were to be the humiliation of a second rejection, he could always leave Hertfordshire behind him forever. He rested his hand against the wall. No, that would ruin any chance he had of persuading her if she were still unsure; and if she refused him, he would never forgive himself for failing to have the patience to wait for a break in the weather.

It was unfair that Bingley had the right to spend his entire day at Longbourn in the company of his beloved Jane, whereas Darcy had to limit himself to brief social calls, then return alone to Netherfield and face his unpleasant thoughts. It probably appeared odd enough that he was calling every day.

On the seventh day Mrs. Bennet invited him to stay for dinner. It was a casual invitation, clearly aimed at pleasing Bingley rather than out of any desire for Darcy's company, but he seized the opportunity to extend his visit. At least he could enjoy watching Elizabeth, even if they could not talk privately.

Dinner started out propitiously, as he was seated next to Elizabeth. Perhaps that was a good sign. Surely they would have some conversation now. If only her presence did not make it so difficult for him to think about anything except the curve of her neck, the scent of rosewater, and how her lips would taste.

He forced his mind back to more innocent topics. "I received a letter from my sister yesterday. She asked me to give you her regards."

Elizabeth's smile drew his attention back to her rosy lips. "Is she still at Pemberley?"

"Yes; though she wrote last that she wished she could join me here. She regrets that your acquaintance was interrupted, and hopes to have the opportunity to resume it in the future." It was a slight exaggeration of what Georgiana had written, but he was certain the sentiment was accurate. He kept a close eye on Elizabeth to judge her response.

That blush again. "I wish it might prove to be the case. She is a delightful young lady."

"Mr. and Mrs. Gardiner are very amiable company as well. I was glad to have the opportunity to meet them."

She looked up at him with that arch look he loved so well. He was so enchanted he almost missed what she said. "I understand you had the opportunity to dine with them in London as well."

Her words took a moment to sink in, then he felt his palms grow warm. How did she know of that; and if she knew that much, what else might she know? Surely her aunt and uncle were not so little to be trusted! "Indeed I had that pleasure." He could tell she was amused by his sudden discomfiture. "I understand you have often visited there as well."

"I always enjoy visiting *Cheapside*."

He let out a breath of relief. If she was teasing him, it could not be all bad. "The company there is excellent."

Her eyes turned down again. "I believe they have much to

be *grateful* for." Then she surprised him by looking up at him. "As do we all."

She knew. But what did she think, and more importantly, what did she feel? Now even if she accepted him, he would never know whether it was for love or from a sense of obligation. Even the sight of her fine eyes could not make up for the disappointment.

He took a sip of wine to cover his confusion. "Gratitude is sometimes given where it is not deserved. I hope it would give no one any unease."

She raised her eyebrows. "Mr. Darcy?"

"Yes, Miss Elizabeth?"

She glanced beyond him meaningfully. "The potatoes."

He looked to his other side and found her sister Mary holding a dish of potatoes with an air of saintly patience. He was making a fine fool of himself tonight. He took them from her with a word of thanks, then held the dish for Elizabeth. She served herself; then, as she placed the spoon back in the dish, she paused for a moment, caught his eye, and brushed the back of her hand against his as she sat back.

It could have been accidental except for her look. He stared at her in astonishment, completely oblivious to the rest of the company, his hand burning where hers had touched it. That settled it. He *would* drag her bodily out of the company and propose to her. At least, that was what he would do if his hands were not full with a dish of potatoes.

A sly smile curled his lips as he realized she was as discomfited as he. "Miss Elizabeth?"

"Yes, Mr. Darcy?"

"The potatoes."

There it was again, that arch smile. "Of course. How thoughtless of me." She reached for the dish, but he did not release it to her until his fingertips had caressed hers for the briefest of moments. The shock of the exquisite sensation of touching her at last, even in such a limited fashion, was enough to make him catch his breath. By the flush on her face, he was sure Elizabeth was similarly affected.

But the sparkle never left her fine eyes. "Mr. Darcy, I understand you are travelling to London tomorrow. I hope the rain will not make for an uncomfortable journey."

He dragged himself back from his contemplation of her beauty, hoping he could manage to sound at least somewhat sensible. "I believe that leaving my friends in Hertfordshire will be a greater source of discomfort than the rain. Fortunately, I will return in but a few days' time."

"I hope you will be back in time to attend next week's assembly." She gave him a look through her lashes.

"I would not miss it for the world. But since I may not return until the day before the assembly, would it be too forward to request now the honour of the first dances of the evening?" He waited in painful anticipation of her answer, knowing it would signify more than an acceptance as a dance partner.

She tilted her head to the side, a teasing gleam in her fine eyes. "I am sure I would find the prospect *tolerable* enough to tempt me, though perhaps not everyone would share my opinion."

He leaned toward her and spoke quietly, for her ears only. "If you wish to discuss the subject of temptation, I should be more than happy to, since I have recently made quite a study of it."

Her mouth dropped open at his blatant flirtation. "Why, Mr. Darcy, I cannot imagine what you mean."

He eyed her significantly. "Perhaps we can discuss the matter in more detail on my return."

Elizabeth had dressed with more than usual care for the assembly.

She had hopes that Mr. Darcy might take the opportunity to converse with her, possibly even to declare himself. It seemed ironic that this might take place in the same setting in which, little over a year earlier, he had declared her not handsome enough to tempt him.

She missed his company as well. She had hoped he would call that morning, but Bingley had come alone, saying that Mr. Darcy had been delayed, but should be arriving later today. Her lips curved with anticipation of seeing him again.

He was not at the assembly when she arrived. Two gentlemen asked her for the favour of the first dance, and she had explained it was already promised. The rest of her dance card filled quickly. She had hoped to save another dance in case Mr. Darcy should ask her for one, but she could not refuse one gentleman and then later accept Mr. Darcy. She wished he had not timed his arrival so late; they might have had the opportunity to talk before the dancing began. But as the musicians began to tune their instruments, she began to wonder if he would claim his promised dance at all. Till she saw Mr. Bingley and his sisters arrive without him, a doubt of his being present had never occurred to her. But in an instant arose the dreadful suspicion that something other than a delay accounted for his absence.

Perhaps his journey to London had allowed him the time to reflect on the disadvantages of an alliance with her, those arguments his aunt had no doubt presented to him. He had not seemed discouraged by it before, but she might have read too much into his behaviour. Or perhaps he had seen her as a challenge, and once he assured himself that her affections were his for the asking, he had lost interest.

As the first dance formed up, one of the gentlemen whose invitation she had refused looked at her askance, clearly of the opinion she had been toying with him by saying the dance was promised. Bingley was partnered with Jane, so she could not turn to her sister for comfort. The music struck up and the dancers began to move. Elizabeth's every prospect of enjoyment of the evening was destroyed. How could she find any pleasure in the later dances, knowing what she had lost?

Wishing to avoid any more curious eyes, she fled to on the dressing rooms in the public part of the inn, where she might unleash her imagination in private. She did not emerge until the first set was nearly ended. Hoping against hope that Darcy might have arrived in her absence, she searched the room for him in vain.

She managed to put on a pretence of enjoyment for her partner in the second set. If she did not think of her disappointment, perhaps no one else would realize it either. She had deliberately avoided Jane between the dances; it would not do for her sister to know that her betrothed's friend had jilted her sister. Better Jane should think Darcy of no importance to Elizabeth. She refused to allow herself to wonder if she would ever see him again.

She was circling her partner in the third set when she caught a glimpse of dark hair. Her breath caught in her throat, but she reminded herself that he had not come for the dance he had promised her, and it might have been a deliberate avoidance. With her partner, she walked down the line of dancers. Until she reached the head of the line again, Darcy would be hidden from view.

The dance, although one she normally enjoyed, seemed to take forever. Elizabeth tried to school herself not to watch for him as she reached the head of the line, but he proved impossible to miss, since he was looking straight at her. His expression was brooding. She felt his eyes on her, and was grateful that the dance gave her an excuse for looking flushed.

The dance ended, leaving her with the decision of whether she dared approach Darcy herself. Her heart told her to, but propriety spoke otherwise. Instead, she chose an intermediate course and made her way to the refreshment table not far from where he stood. For that she needed no excuse.

She felt rather than saw him come up beside her, but she did not look up at him until he spoke her name. Surely he would not make a point of seeking her out if his wishes had changed.

"Please allow me to express my deepest apologies for my late arrival. The bridge was washed out and the river half in flood – all the rain, you know. I had to ride miles upstream to find a ford that was passable. I came as quickly as I could." The deep regret in his expression could not be mistaken.

"I certainly cannot hold you responsible for the vagaries of the weather or of the roads."

"You are very kind. Would it be too much to hope that I might claim a different dance, even though I missed my first opportunity?"

"I wish I could oblige you, but I fear my dance card is already full." Why, oh why, had so many men asked her to dance tonight?

"I see." It was clear by the set of his jaw that he did not like what he saw.

Just then her next partner approached her and offered her his arm. Elizabeth gave Darcy a regretful glance as she departed.

The next dance was a lively one, and her partner amiable, but she could not help being aware of Darcy watching her. He stood alone by the wall, wearing a slight scowl which lightened only when he caught her eye. She found it difficult to look away, even as the dance took her from him.

After circling half-way around the room, she looked up from the dance again, but he was no longer where he had been. She scanned the crowd as she passed her partner by the hand, hoping he would not notice her distraction. She finally saw Darcy's tall form standing next to her father, apparently engaged in serious conversation with him. As if they sensed her glance, both men looked in her direction, then turned to each other again.

So Darcy was not going to wait for an answer from her. Elizabeth's pulses fluttered at the thought of what he must be saying. What would her father think? Would he give his permission without asking her consent? Her cheeks grew hot at the thought that by the time she left the dance floor, she might well be engaged to Mr. Darcy.

The two men were still conversing when the dance ended. Elizabeth tried to make her feet move in their direction, but they were frozen to the floor. It was not as if she had any intention of denying his suit, but now that the reality was before her, she felt such embarrassment that she could not imagine looking him in the face. In a moment of sheer cowardice, she fled the hall and hid once again in a dressing room.

Once alone, she pressed her hands to her flushed cheeks. It was not like her to be so *Missish,* but then again she had never before been faced with the immediate prospect of being engaged. She imagined how Darcy would look at her, now that he knew she would be his someday, and it made heat rise within her.

But she could not hide forever. She took a deep breath before opening the door and proceeding down the long hallway to the assembly room. She was grateful it was unpopulated at present; she did not feel equal to making casual conversation.

"Miss Elizabeth." The deep voice of the object of her thoughts came from behind her.

She jumped and held her hand to her chest, her heart pounding. "You startled me, sir."

"Indeed." The corner of his mouth twitched wryly. He glanced up and down the hallway, then placed a firm hand on her elbow and directed her through an open door into an unoccupied room.

Quickly he closed the door behind them, and suddenly Elizabeth could see nothing but blackness. She was all too aware of his on her arm.

"My apologies. I had assumed there would be light from the street."

Her eyes, adjusting to the darkness, made out the window frame, with only the light of the stars to fill it. The clouds must have finally cleared. "I believe we are facing the rear of the inn, sir." She could just begin to see the outlines of the room. To her dismay, she realized this was not one of the sitting rooms; instead, she was standing directly between Mr. Darcy and a large four-poster bed. She was grateful he could not see her flaming cheeks.

She took a few quick steps toward the window, seeking to put distance between her and the bed. Not that she doubted Mr. Darcy's honour, but if they were accidentally discovered, she did not want it to look worse than it was. But what was she thinking? If she were found alone with Mr. Darcy in a dark bedroom, it would make no difference whether he was taking advantage of her or they were discussing the weather. The damage would be done. Still, she had never before been alone in a bedroom with a gentleman, and it made her nervous.

She took another step away, but stumbled over some unseen object on the floor. Immediately Mr. Darcy was beside her, supporting her arms.

"Are you hurt, Miss Elizabeth?" His concern was evident.

"Only my dignity is wounded." Her dignity and her reputation, if they were discovered, but somehow she found herself unable to care as he stood so close to her, only an inch or two of air separating them. His hands remained above her elbows, covering the small span between her gloves and the puffed sleeve of her dress, and her eyes opened wide as his thumbs stroked the sensitive skin of her inner arms. Did he have any idea what he was doing to her?

"My apologies." His voice sounded unusually husky. "I did not wish to miss my dance with you."

She struggled to collect herself. "You are forgiven, sir. I am sure there will be another opportunity."

"I hope so, although sometimes I think the fates are as much against allowing me to dance with you as allowing me to be alone with you."

It seemed unwise to point out that they were alone now, especially when she was feeling the light touch of his thumbs throughout her body. "Mr. Darcy, my partner will be looking for me."

"Let him look."

"But what if he begins a search and we are discovered?"

"So much the better."

"Mr. Darcy!"

"If the entire world, including the weather, will insist on conspiring against finding an opportunity to speak with you alone, why should I not simply let events take their course?"

"Surely you cannot mean…."

His fingers crept under the ruffle of her sleeve. "I see three choices before you. One is that I ask your father for permission to court you. Or I could ask for permission to marry you. Or I could keep you here until we are discovered, and wait for him to demand that I marry you. Any of the three are agreeable to me, so you may choose."

"You are all kindness, Mr. Darcy," she murmured. She could feel the warmth of his breath against her cheek, and suddenly she ached for more.

"That does not answer my question." His lips brushed against the corner of her jaw, so lightly it was like a butterfly's touch. But a butterfly would not send shivers of pleasure through her.

"I thought you had already spoken to my father."

"Tonight? True, but we were speaking of books. I thought I should have at least one ordinary conversation with him before demanding his daughter's hand."

She almost laughed at his choice of words. "In that case, it would seem that I have in fact only two options, since you seem disinclined to unhand me. I could wait to see what transpires, or I could scream for help."

Now she felt the warmth of his lips on her brow. "Be warned, Miss Bennet, that should you decide to scream, I would feel obligated to stop you in the most efficient manner possible." His caressing tone told her he did not refer to putting his hand over her mouth.

A wave of dizziness washed over her. Surely he would not dare, yet he had already dared so much. The wisest course would be to accept him officially – he could have no real doubt at this point as to her consent – but then he might stop this sweet torment of closeness. As if aware of her thoughts, his grip on her arms loosened. But it was replaced by the lightest of touches trailing up her arm, a sense both exhilarating and irresistible.

She drew in a ragged breath. "Perhaps you should speak to my father."

She could not make out his hands in the darkness, so she gasped in surprise at his touch on the sensitive skin of her neck, tracing her collarbone.

He moved fractionally closer to her, sending the tension even higher. "Pity. I was hoping you might scream." His hand moved again. This time his fingertips lingered on her tingling lips.

"I still might. Perhaps you should assume the worst." What was wrong with her? She knew better than to allow the intoxication of the moment to go any further. If she reacted this fervently already, how would she possibly manage if he kissed her?

She could feel him leaning toward her, his breath on her cheek.

"I have waited so long for this." His whisper was unsteady, but the pressure of his lips on hers was tender and warm.

Her eyelids fluttered closed. All of her being seemed to her to be concentrated at that point where their mouths met. The rest of the world vanished, and his lips were her only reality.

But then it changed. It was a moment before she felt the teasing touch of his tongue tracing along her lips. The surprise of it made her gasp, the intimacy of it causing her to clutch his shoulders for support. Despite all the novels she had read, she had never imagined such delight in a man's touch.

It only grew as his arms went around her, pulling her to him until she could feel the strength of his body against hers. In a rush of happiness she knew *this* was where she belonged, *this* was what she had been seeking all her life.

His lips pressed against her cheek, her ear, and feathered along the pulse of her neck. "Sweetest, loveliest Elizabeth," he whispered between kisses.

Somehow she found herself standing on her tiptoes, her hands creeping around his neck to clutch him tightly, unable to bear the thought of losing contact with him. Intoxicated by the faint scent of leather and horses that clung to him, she pressed her cheek against the starched cloth of his cravat, feeling half unable to breathe for happiness.

Jane's distant voice calling her name barely penetrated her dazed state, but Darcy stiffened, still holding her close. "They have missed you, my love," he said. With clear regret he loosened his grip on her. "You must go. I will remain here a few minutes, and *then* I will speak to your father."

Finally Bingley looked as if he was ready to depart. It was not a moment too soon. Darcy had reached the end of his tolerance for sharing Elizabeth with the rest of the Meryton assembly. Turning to Elizabeth, he offered her his arm and said, "Miss Elizabeth, your father has agreed to allow me the honour of escorting you home this evening."

"You have been planning ahead, sir." Her eyes danced as she took his arm.

"It seems I must, if I am to have any time with you at all."

"I am surprised he agreed to allow me to travel alone with you."

"Well, I might perhaps have implied we would be riding with Bingley, your sister, and Miss Bingley." He led her outside to the street where he paused a moment to look up at the sky. "*Now* it stops raining." Just when it no longer made a difference.

His carriage waited in line behind several others. Darcy placed his free hand over Elizabeth's. Walking perhaps a little closer to her than propriety would dictate, he guided her to it, opened the door, and handed her in. To think he would have the opportunity to do this again and again throughout their lives! It still astonished him that after all these months, it was finally settled, and Elizabeth was to be his.

He needed to rein his thoughts in before they could travel any further in that direction, or there would be a repeat of his uncontrolled behaviour earlier when he had been alone with Elizabeth. He stepped into the carriage and seated himself opposite her, then rapped on the wall of the carriage to signal the coachman. As the steady clip-clop of hooves on cobblestones began, he leaned forward to speak to Elizabeth.

"I hope you do not object to my maneuvering for a little time alone with you. I wanted the opportunity to apologize for my earlier behaviour. I had been awaiting that moment so long, and I fear my emotions ran too high."

There was a low laugh from the dim shape that was Elizabeth. "You need not apologize. You knew I planned to accept you, and you expressed yourself as sensibly as a man violently in love can be supposed to do on such an occasion."

He only wished he had been certain of her acceptance, but at Hunsford he had no doubts of her, and could not have been more mistaken. The indications she had recently given him of her regard had raised his hopes, but he had not been complacent until she had spoken the words. "I thank you for your understanding, but still, I would like to think I have a little more self-control than that."

Elizabeth reached across the divide and took his hand. Obviously she had no conception of how slight his self-control with her actually was. "Sir, I was grateful for the reassurance of your affections. You had seemed less than pleased before that, and I was concerned as to the meaning of it."

"My dearest Elizabeth, you cannot expect me to enjoy the sight of you dancing with other gentlemen when I could not look forward to the same pleasure for myself." He felt the warmth of her hand through the thin white glove she wore. It reminded him too much of the sensation of kissing her. Perhaps this carriage ride had not been such a good idea after all. Unable to resist, he ran his thumb lightly down the inside of her forefinger, thinking of the day when he would have the right to strip off her gloves, to press kisses on each fingertip and to trace with his lips the fine lines of her hands that he had so admired on the keyboard at Rosings. Then he would... but no. He could not allow his thoughts to go there. "But since our time together earlier was so brief, I did not have the opportunity to tell you how very happy you have made me, and how much I look forward to the day when I may call you my wife." No. He should not have said that last part.

"I confess I have been able to think of little else myself," she said, and he could almost make out the arch smile which accompanied her words.

Did she have any idea how much of a temptation she presented? He needed to change the subject before he gave into it. "Your father was more surprised by my petition than I had anticipated."

"But no doubt less surprised than he might have been a fortnight ago, before you began to call at Longbourn so regularly."

"Perhaps I should have waited until I could speak to him in greater privacy, but I am afraid my impatience had the better of me."

"Well, all's well that ends well." Her hand tightened on his. "My early impressions of you have been proven to be quite mistaken. To think I once thought you to have a taciturn and unsociable disposition! Now there are times when I must say that you *talk* altogether too much, Mr. Darcy. It will not take us long to reach Longbourn at this pace."

His eyebrows shot up in surprise. No one had ever accused him of being too talkative before. What did she expect him to do, if not to talk to her? Suddenly it occurred to him precisely what she expected him to do, and a great sense of lightness pervaded his being. Not to mention other feelings for the altogether astonishing woman he was to marry.

He shifted his weight and crossed the narrow space between them to sit at her side, his arm finding its way around her shoulders almost of its own accord. "In that case, my sweetest Elizabeth, I must find a better way to express myself."

The taste of her lips was sweet indeed.

# Acknowledgements

This book could not have been written without the assistance of many people, first and foremost my husband David who has cheerfully supported my odd hobby for years. Special thanks to reader Arlene Brown who suggested the title and to Rebecca Young for her opinion on cover art. My fellow Austen Authors have provided encouragement, enthusiasm, and lots of good reading to distract me.

# About the Author

Abigail Reynolds is a lifelong Jane Austen enthusiast and a physician. In addition to writing, she has a part-time private practice and enjoys spending time with her family. Originally from upstate New York, she studied Russian, theater, and marine biology at Bryn Mawr College before deciding to attend medical school. She began writing *PRIDE & PREJUDICE* variations in 2001 to spend more time with her very favorite characters. Encouragement from fellow Austen fans convinced her to continue asking 'What if…?', which led to six other Pemberley Variations and her modern novel, *THE MAN WHO LOVED PRIDE & PREJUDICE*. She is currently at work on another Pemberley Variation and sequels to *THE MAN WHO LOVED PRIDE & PREJUDICE*.

Abigail is a founding member of Austen Authors (www.austenauthors.com), a popular group blog comprising twenty-five authors of Austenesque fiction. Her website, www.pemberleyvariations.com, has more information on upcoming books. Abigail is a lifetime member of JASNA and lives in Wisconsin with her husband, two children, and a menagerie of wild animals masquerading as pets. Her hobbies include beading, reading, and finding time to sleep.

Made in the USA
Lexington, KY
14 May 2011